CW01501260

A Battle of Lo
Dark Sapphic Romance
By Mia M.R

Trigger warnings may include but are not limited to: Violence and gore, mild dub-con, swearing, extreme jealousy, and obsessive behaviour. .

The Heart of a Demon series

The most beautiful rose often has the sharpest thorns.

Blurb

With her sweet Angel by her side, life for Lilith is as close to perfect as it gets. But when she is summoned to Hell by her life-long friend and Master, Lilith realises that love and jealousy are powerful motivators for betrayal.

Heartbroken and enraged, Lilith's desires turn dark and murderous, threatening to rekindle the ancient war and bring chaos to Heaven, Hell, and the mortal realm.

Chapter 1

"Oh, shit!" Eden exclaimed, before a hand reached out from behind to muffle the cry. She groaned and dug her fingers into the chipped wood of the nameless professor's desk, desperately trying not to call her pleasure for all to hear.

"Naughty, pet," Lilith scolded from behind, pushing her fingers into Eden with torturously slow strokes. She raised her hand, and the slap that followed echoed through the empty classroom, leaving a bright red handprint on Eden's shaking behind.

"You try keeping quiet while being bent over a desk and fuck-*ED*," Eden tried to snap, the cry falling into a stuttered yell as Lilith's tail wound between her legs to stroke her aching clit.

Lilith laughed; a sound no less malevolent despite her fondness for the woman clenching around her fingers, and she leaned forward to nibble and bite at the exposed skin of Eden's neck.

Eden spread her legs wider and bucked her hips into the sweet torment of Lilith's thrusts, desperately chasing the high that was so cruelly being denied. The table below groaned its protest at the added weight, but neither woman paid it any mind.

"Oh, but you don't want to keep quiet; do you pet? You want to be discovered. You want someone to catch you being pinned and screwed by the big, bad demon," Lilith taunted, maintaining the same tortuously slow pace.

They could both hear exactly what the words did to Eden; they could both hear the rush of wetness that gathered and pooled between her legs as Lilith drove her relentlessly to the edge of release.

But it wasn't enough, and Lilith knew it.

Eden bit the inside of her cheek and tried to push herself back onto Lilith's fingers, the sound loud and obscene in her ears.

"Give in to me, pet." Lilith demanded, kissing and scratching her nails down Eden's broad back. She could taste the salty sweat on the Angel's back; hear the frantic rushing of blood that pumped through the veins below her teeth, tempting her to bury her fangs into Eden's shoulder and drain her soul dry.

Eden tried to hold out. It was a new game of theirs. She would resist until the very last moment, holding out until tears pricked at her eyes and she couldn't take it a second more, before falling into a fit of shameless pleas.

Their mid-afternoon fuck was met with reluctance at first on Eden's part, a reaction that only inflamed Lilith's desire to take the girl. It wasn't often that the demon interrupted her classes, but when she did, it was a demand, not a request.

Eden broke with a desperate groan, finally melting into her subservient nature with relief as the pleasure became unbearable and overwhelming.

"Please," She pleaded longingly, reaching behind to grip the woman plastered to her back, keeping her prone and bent over the desk.

"Hmm? What was that, pet? I can't seem to hear you," Lilith whispered into her ear, slowing her thrusts even further.

Eden whined, a high-pitched noise that began in her throat and blossomed into the air. "You wicked bitch," she panted, desperately trying to grind herself against the tail flicking between her legs. But it moved away, lazily swatting at her thick, wobbling thighs, and Eden almost screamed her frustration.

"Fuck me, please!" She begged, flattening herself further onto the desk and tilting her neck, fully baring it in submission.

Lilith grinned, her face dark in desire, and she sank her fangs into the plump flesh of Eden's shoulder. As Eden's soul and energy leeched into her, she picked up the pace, curling her fingers with every thrust into the velvet channel clenching around her.

Eden nearly wept in relief and desperately sought to hold onto the rocking desk, lest she be pushed over the top as it moved below her, inching forward under the force of the succubus' thrusts.

"Someone's coming, pet." Lilith warned casually, as if being caught was no issue for her. And it wasn't. She was far too old to worry about a little bit of exhibition, but the sweet Angel moaning below her might not be so blasé about the exposure.

"Please don't stop," Eden eventually groaned, pressing her cheek to the grainy wood below.

Lilith smirked and trailed her tail between Eden's legs once again, rubbing it against the pulsating clit between the Angel's lower lips.

"*Yes, yes, oh yes,*" Eden chanted as she finally tipped over the edge and into ecstasy. She released a guttural moan, slumping onto the desk, panting, and gasping for breath as Lilith sucked marks into the flesh of her neck.

"Such a good girl for me," the succubus praised, lowering herself to her knees to drag her tongue through Eden's dripping folds.

Lilith didn't let a drop go to waste, and Eden fought to remain still and not jolt away as the demon's tongue dragged across her oversensitive flesh.

Lilith would punish her if she tried to deny her, so Eden lay moaning and boneless, draped over the desk like a well- used whore. Which is exactly what she was, a fact that warmed her from within.

Lilith licked higher and spread Eden's cheeks, lingering just below the tight ring of muscles that clenched uneasily at the nearness. She had been teasing and toying with the act for a while, slowly easing Eden into the idea and steadily building her pet's confidence. Eden's comfort was rarely her first concern when it came to sex, but she wasn't a complete brute.

Eden tensed, anxiously biting her lip as Lilith lingered, and she sighed with relief when the demon abandoned her teasing to pull her underwear and trousers back up her legs. It was something new that Lilith had taken to doing after fucking her. The succubus seemed to delight in re-dressing her, as if she were a present to unwrap later.

"You can pay me back later," Lilith purred, the words hot and heavy in her ear, bordering between a promise and a threat. She wrenched Eden's head back, twisting it painfully so that they could kiss. Eden eagerly met the woman's lips, moaning at the taste of herself on Lilith's tongue, and she smiled at the deceptively sweet caresses lingering on her sides.

The door opened, and Eden pushed herself away from the desk on unsteady legs. Professor Milton stepped through, shrewdly eyeing her unkempt appearance and mussed hair. But Lilith was already gone, so Eden only smiled sweetly and subtly wiped the remains of her cum from the desk.

"May I help you?" He asked, his eyes darting around the room. It stank of sweat and sex, and the glazed, almost zombie-like look on the student's face was unmistakable. But no one else was here, so Milton dismissed his suspicion and frowned at the young woman.

"No, thank you, professor. My apologies: I thought this was Ethics," Eden lied breathlessly, even as a pink blush rose on her rounded cheeks.

Professor Milton rolled his eyes; this was the third time in a month that Eden had mistaken his classroom. Perhaps he should find the girl a map.

"As always, Miss Waif, next class along," he informed her impatiently, eager to begin his lunch break.

Eden nodded and giggled, rushing from the room on unsteady legs. "Do you think he knows?" She whispered, knowing her demon would hear.

"*He suspects,*" Lilith replied in that odd way of hers that no one else could hear. "*He's quite feminine for a man; perhaps one day I'll let him catch us.*"

Eden screwed up her nose and shook her head at the spectre of Lilith's voice. "Please don't," she whispered back, ever mindful of the others traversing the halls around her. Lilith laughed wickedly into her ear, unheard by everyone else.

"*Don't you worry, pet. I don't like to share my things.*"

Eden smiled softly. The possessive statement would've made many run for the hills, but it only made her heart bloom with warmth.

Eden belonged to Lilith, in every way possible.

"Can we go flying later?" She murmured under her breath as she took her seat, in the correct classroom this time, and pulled out her laptop.

"*If you wish,*" Lilith said, her voice caressing the shell of Eden's ear, bringing goosebumps to her skin and shivers to her form.

The laptop was a lot nicer than the last one. It was compact and sleek, holding near unlimited memory, and in her bag, Eden had her own portable Wi-Fi box, so she didn't need to connect to the crappy internet offered by the university. She hadn't even realised that portable WI-FI was a thing. The stupid shit money could buy, she thought with a shrug.

Accepting the gifts made Eden a little uncomfortable, but Lilith had looked so terribly pleased with herself for taking care of 'her Angel' that she didn't feel it wise to refuse.

Lilith may have endless experience with sex, but when it came to the more complicated matters of a relationship, she could get a little…

sensitive. And by sensitive, Eden meant intense, misguided, and sometimes a little terrifying.

She also held absolutely no concept of what was considered expensive, something that grated on Eden's instinctually frugal nature.

Eden shifted in her seat, mindful of the pleasant discomfort and lingering ache between her legs as it pulsed from within, treating her to a reminder of their recent activities. Honestly, she couldn't remember the last time she wasn't at least a little bit sore down there.

A notification popped up, and Eden didn't even think before clicking on it. Her eyes widened, her body practically blushing from head to toe at the suggestive image displayed on the screen.

"Couldn't wait one fucking hour," she muttered, more frustrated than annoyed. The image of Lilith's hand between her spread legs, her pressed shirt parted to reveal her breasts as she fingered herself, was going to live rent-free in her mind for the remainder of the lesson.

Eden did her best to turn her attention to the teacher. She only had one more year to go. After that, freedom. To do what, she wasn't entirely sure.

Her life over the last few months had revolved around going to class, getting fucked, and trying not to be murdered.

Despite their victory against the Knight of Hell, demons seemed to be crawling out of the woodwork, appearing from thin air in an attempt to be the one to slay, or even just look, upon an Angel. An action that ultimately resulted in their destruction at Lilith's hand.

Unfortunately for Eden, she didn't seem to possess many qualities of her heavenly heritage. Lilith had told her that every Angel possessed a gift; something to help them fulfil their 'purpose.' But no matter how hard she tried, she'd been unable to recreate the force that had brought Egan to his knees and burnt his flesh.

Flying was about all she had, and while Eden adored soaring through the clouds, she couldn't help but be a little disappointed.

The Angels on her favourite TV shows all got cool powers like freezing time, healing, or mind reading. She felt a little lacking in comparison.

Chapter 2

"Damn!" Eden cursed when Lilith once again escaped her clutches. They were soaring high above the clouds, through the frigid wind that whipped hair around her face and made her teeth chatter. The sheer height of the fall made her heart pound in exhilaration, daring her to spin and dip, playing in the rapidly shifting air current that threatened to send her spinning to the ground at any moment.

Lilith laughed and swooped under her, the ginormous wings attached to her back creating a strong draft that Eden struggled not to fall into.

"Oh, pet, you can do better than that," the demon mocked. She glided lazily under the Angel, her hand reaching up to squeeze Eden's ankle as she once more evaded the girl's reaching hands.

The small touch softened Eden's annoyance, and she poked her tongue out at the demon lingering below.

"Careful, or I might put that tongue to good use and really test your flight skills," Lilith threatened, winking up at her.

Eden hastily pulled her tongue back into her mouth; she had no doubt that Lilith would follow through on the threat. Wondering about the logistics of having sex on a cloud, Eden grinned and pulled a face at the back of the demon's head as the woman flew beneath her.

Lilith remained just out of arms reach, never venturing far from Eden's clumsy flight, something that should've given her an advantage. But really, Eden was as uncoordinated in the sky as she was on the ground. Hence the reason Lilith stayed close.

The last time she'd strayed too far, a sudden breeze had caught the girl's wings, sending her spinning out of control. And while Lilith had found it pretty funny, Eden hadn't quite shared her humour after plummeting into a lake. So, she watched diligently, her face the very picture of indulgence as the Angel's confidence slowly grew in the sky.

The English countryside, or what Eden could see of it through the thick cloud cover, sprawled out below them, seemingly endless. To the east, London, and Eden's hopeful destination in the following weeks. Now all she had to do was convince Lilith to come with her, though Eden was quite certain a little bribery would work wonders.

Lilith was a creature who thrived in hedonism, indulging in her every whim and desire with barely a thought to those around her. Something that had brought Eden no end of embarrassment after being caught in several *compromising* positions, but it did make for an easy method of getting whatever she wanted.

"Lilly?" Eden called through a yawn that threatened to unhinge her jaw. Flying was hard work, and while her wings still grew in power and strength, she tired quickly.

Lilith glided closer to take Eden into her arms. The brief touch of the Angel's wings stung, but Eden quickly pulled them back into her body so that she could curl into Lilith's hold and rest her head on her breast. A rumbling purr vibrated in the demon's chest, a new phenomenon that Eden obviously loved but irritated Lilith to no end.

'I'm not a bloody cat,' Lilith would often mutter as the Angel teased and stroked her hair, tugging on her tail and comparing her to Maxx. An action that would usually result in the Angel pinned and spread, screaming obscenities as she endured Lilith's wicked attentions.

With Eden in her grip and no longer at risk of crash landing, Lilith sped through the sky, flying faster than most mortals could see. Her tail curled around her body, wrapping around Eden's calf, stroking up and down in a soothing motion as the Angel became limp and heavy in her grip.

The city came back into view, and Lilith eyed it with irritation. Previously attracting little interest from the supernatural world, it was now a hotbed for demonic activity.

Nymphs had started appearing, taking over the few green spaces and parks throughout the area. Living gargoyles stood stationed throughout the city, harmless and uninterested in the mortals who awed over the new pieces of street 'art.'

But Lilith knew what they were here for.

As benign as some of these creatures usually were, they all came running to the sweet siren call of Eden's angelic presence. A presence that grew by the day and set Lilith's teeth on edge.

She'd contemplated just abducting her lover and flying to some remote island in the middle of the god-damned ocean. No doubt Eden would pout and seethe for a bit, but Lilith was more than capable of keeping her Angel distracted.

Landing on the roof, Lilith abruptly dropped Eden onto the sun lounger, grinning playfully when the sleepy Angel yelped and glowered up at her, grumbling curses under her breath. She manhandled Eden into a more comfortable position, settling in beside her to bask in the remaining sunlight streaming through the clouds.

Thankfully, she couldn't tan, but the warmth on her skin felt wonderful.

Eden shifted to sit cross-legged by Lilith's side, lazily playing with the demonic tail wrapped around her ankle, laughing quietly when it started twitching away and gently batting at her fingers.

Apparently, the appendage was one great, big erogenous zone. Something that Eden was embarrassed to learn when she'd begun playing with it in a crowded club.

"Lilly," a sweetly demanding voice wavered by Lilith's ear. "Stay here, pet." She said with a roll of her eyes and a sigh.

Eden watched the succubus leave with a faint frown on her lips. Jealousy coiled in her chest, but she pushed the feeling away, reminding herself that the demon was hers alone, no matter what the Devil seemed to think.

The second Lilith stepped out of the sunlight; Lucifer materialised in the shadows. "Glorious," they practically moaned, running their ghostly touch over her skin and parting her shirt.

Lilith huffed as the buttons popped, exposing her to their grasping hands. There was nothing genuinely sexual about the touch. Lucy had never expressed any true interest in her, but they enjoyed pushing her buttons too much to stop. Their gaze was akin to an artist marvelling at their finest creation, proudly drinking in her radiance, in awe of her very existence.

Maxx, the skeletal monstrosity that was her cat, slinked out of Lilith's bedroom to glower up at the pair. He hissed, growling at the spectre touching his mistress as he made his way up to the roof. The little traitor adored Eden; practically followed her around like a second shadow. He seemed to feed off the Angel's discontent, and got increasingly grumpy every time Lucifer made an appearance.

"To what do I owe the pleasure, my friend?" Lilith asked, examining the purple tips of her nails. Two were cut shorter than the rest, for obvious reasons. While her claws were retractable, only growing into sharp, deadly talons when the need arose, she still made sure to keep her nails trimmed to suit Eden's comfort in the bedroom. The poor Angel did not quite have Lilith's healing capabilities, or her pain tolerance.

"Can I not just pop in to visit my favourite succubus?" Satan asked in mock offence, dramatically clutching a shadowy hand to their chest.

Lilith looked at them wryly, playfully blowing a sharp gust of formless magic from her lips, and she grinned as their visage scattered and reformed.

"You always have a reason," she said dryly. "Even if it's only to torment me." Or my pet, she thought. But she would not bring up Eden. Lucy was getting increasingly pouty over the Angel's presence.

Satan grinned and draped themself over Lilith's couch, stretching out like a satisfied cat. They crooked a finger, summoning her to their side. "I need you to come to hell sooner than expected." They said, frustrating Lilith further.

"I agreed to visit soon. We are immortal; soon could be a century from now," she argued tightly, a deep frown appearing between her brows.

In truth, she didn't want to leave Eden. Her pet was so very vulnerable, and if she left for any length of time, Lilith feared the Angel would not be here when she returned. Time worked differently in Hell, a mere hour there could range from a minute to a day on earth.

"It *could*, but it won't be," Lucy cooed, pushing an undercurrent of authority into their voice.

"What need do you have of me?" Lilith asked shortly, seething at the overstep into her time as she tensed under the imitation of hands brushing over her thighs. She forced herself to relax; forced herself to try and take part in the game they had been playing since almost the dawn of time.

But her heart wasn't in it.

No, what little was left of Lilith's heart lay upstairs, contained within the Angel sprawled out on the roof, awaiting her return.

Lucy sensed her disinterest in the play and hissed their disapproval. Their grip did not tighten; they did not hurt her, but the shadows that made up their hands grew sharp in their irritation as they dragged over her skin.

Lilith swallowed the growl building in her chest and unfurled her wings, pushing Lucifer away. But even as she did so, she allowed her shirt to drop open to display the sides of her breasts, knowing it would appease her master.

Lucy didn't look; the flesh itself wasn't what they were interested in. It was the prolonging of their game, the constant push and pull of power that the Devil craved from her.

Lucifer's sharp touch softened again, and they moulded themselves to her back. "I am in need of a champion," they whispered, their words barely more than a wisp of wind on Lilith's ear.

Lilith whipped her head around to narrow her eyes on the spectre of her friend. "What of Crowley?" She asked bitingly.

The pair didn't exactly see eye to eye, especially when it came to the protection of their master. But at the very least, the brute made a halfway decent champion.

Lucifer scoffed and nuzzled into her hair, only to pick their head up at the sound of the door above opening and the heavy patter of Eden's feet coming down the stairs.

"Lilith?" Eden called, knowing full well she was interrupting something.

"I rethink my desire for you to protect her every second," the Devil growled darkly in response. When Eden was just Lilith's plaything, they hadn't given two shits about the Angel. But more and more often lately, they found themself in a petty battle against the woman for Lilith's attention.

Lilith smirked despite herself.

It was exactly in her nature to adore the jealousy and subtle war being waged over her affection, even the pair were getting dangerously close to stepping on her last fucking nerve.

"In here, pet." She called back.

Eden turned the corner, only to freeze at the sight before her. She attempted to reign in her anger, but it still slipped out in the narrowing of her eyes and the tick that appeared in her jaw. Maxx yowled when Eden tightened her grip around his skeletal form, grinding the bones together as he wiggled to free himself.

"Sorry buddy," she murmured, lowering him to the floor. She tried to stay calm; she really, *really* did. But the sight of the Devil draped over *her* demon, caressing skin that belonged solely to Eden, made her burn in fury. It probably wouldn't smart quite so much if Lilith didn't look so pleased with the attention.

Lucy tutted and switched to the demonic tongue. "*Tell your toy to leave, or I will put on a show she won't soon forget,*" they threatened, lowering their hand to Lilith's thigh.

The succubus was caught between a rock and a hard place. If she refused and allowed Eden to stay, Lucifer would make them both regret it. But if she dismissed the Angel, then she held no doubt that she could be in for a very uncomfortable night. But Eden's safety took priority over her anger, a newfound desire that made Lilith almost as uncomfortable as the shadowy hand inching towards the apex of her thighs.

Lilith blew her lover a kiss. "I won't be long, pet." She said dismissively, waving Eden out of the room and biting back the wince that threated to crease her face.

Eden bit her lip, suppressing the hurt that burned in her chest at the casual gesture. She turned on her heel, stomped back up the stairs, and slammed the door behind her with a loud bang that echoed through the stately apartment.

Lilith sighed and squeezed the bridge of her nose. She hadn't had a headache in... well, ever really. But between these two, she might just be the first immortal to get one.

"Satisfied?" she asked, yanking her shirt closed and stretching out her wings. They shook in agitation, responding to the faint undercurrent of anger exuding off her Master.

"Immensely," Lucy said sarcastically. "You *will* attend to me in hell, Lilith." It was a command from her Master, not a request from her friend.

Lilith ground her teeth and nodded her head. "When?" She asked shortly, eager to be rid of them so that she could return to the Angel she could hear pacing a hole in the roof.

Satan smiled and leaned in to press their lips against the back of her neck, sweetly kissing the pale skin that tightened and tensed under the touch.

"The challenge has been called for the summer solstice. I'm sure you'll be back up here with your little pet in no time," they said, leaving one last lingering touch to Lilith's jaw before disappearing entirely.

"Dramatic little bastard," Lilith groaned.

Maxx glared up at her, his fur-less tail slamming against the hard wood floor. "Oh, don't you fucking start," she snapped, scooping the cat into her arms.

Eden was going to be pissed, and Lilith hoped that the presence of the adorable monstrosity might weaken the girl's ire. Maxx growled and fought the hold, feeding off the Angel's anger, but Lilith only flashed her fangs at the creature until it stilled. "Pet?" She called quietly as she made her way onto the roof.

Eden paused in her pacing, fury tightening the features of her face. She crossed her arms over her breasts and glared at the approaching demon.

Chapter 3

"It really doesn't take him very long, does it? Are you properly satisfied?" Eden mocked, taking a step back for every one that Lilith took towards her.

"Them," Lilith corrected, more out of habit than anything, and nearly winced when Eden's fury went from simmering to a full-on broil.

"For fucks sake, Eden," she eventually snapped, using the Angel's name, which she rarely did. "If you have forgotten, Lucy grants me my power, at least in part. What would you like me to do? Tell them to bugger off because you're a little sensitive about them groping me?" She asked, unleashing a little bit of her own frustration at the situation.

"*YES!*" Eden yelled back, startling the demon as well as the undead cat in her arms. Eden didn't yell, especially at her. Sure, Lilith's eccentricities sometimes grated on her nerves, but she always reacted with barely more than irritated exasperation.

"Do you know how it makes me feel when I walk down those stairs to find the asshole you call 'Master,' draped over you like a cheap necklace?" Eden asked, striking a finger into Lilith's chest.

The demon hissed and reached for her, but Eden was already backing away. Not out of fear, Lilith only hurt her in bed, and only ever in ways Eden enjoyed, but she knew if she allowed Lilith to wrap her arms around her, then her anger would be lost.

"You threatened to rip my friend's heart out because you were jealous, and you *did actually kill her*! And what? I'm not allowed to feel the same?" Eden stressed, her wings unfurling and curling around her form in an effort to keep Lilith from pouncing on her.

Lilith scoffed. Not this again.

"I killed her because she betrayed you." She snapped, her tail whipping from side to side in agitation and all of her unholy additions fully on show.

"You were jealous," Eden countered, shaking her head. "And you used her betrayal as an excuse."

Not one hundred percent accurate, but Lilith couldn't deny that it was a minor factor in her actions. Not that she would admit it.

Having enough of the temper tantrum, Lilith ignored the stinging pain that came from being in contact with Eden's wings, gently forcing them aside to press into the Angel's space.

"Do you not understand how precarious our situation is, you silly girl?" Lilith finally snapped, grasping the furious Angel by her waist and backing her up.

Eden stumbled at the abrupt gesture, but Lilith caught her, not allowing the Angel to fall to her feet.

"It is through their grace that you even live at all. It is their friendship and devotion to me that ensures your safety. So no matter how much it turns your stomach, yes! I *expect* you to accept them, even if you don't like them." Lilith was nearly yelling by the end, her icy blue eyes glinting dangerously, casting an eery blue glow over the roof.

Eden went still under her hands and looked away, not out of submission, but rather, to hide her tears.

"I'm sorry–" Lilith went to say, knowing that she'd crossed a line in her frustration. Eden didn't allow her to finish the apology. The Angel leaned in, stealing her breath with a passionate kiss and tangling her hands into Lilith's thick, dark hair.

"I cannot stand it. Their hands on you, their lips, it is *infuriating*," Eden whispered against her mouth, the last word barely more than a growl.

Lilith moaned at the feeling of Eden's tongue brushing against her own. She reached down to pick the Angel up, forcing her to hook her legs around her waist. For a mortal, Eden's weight would make such a feat difficult, but Lilith knew the show of strength would only inflame her arousal.

As irritating as the petty battle between the two was getting, Lilith had to admit that the furious sex it resulted in was more than satisfying.

"I'm yours, pet," she murmured against Eden's jaw, loving every little gasp and moan that slipped free as she squeezed and palmed the Angel's ass.

They were words that she had spoken to no other, including her master. It was startling every time they slipped from her lips, mostly because Lilith didn't realise how true they were until she was saying them.

"Prove it," Eden demanded, a sudden challenge in her eyes as she pulled her shirt over her head, throwing it to the floor with barely a glance.

Lilith raised an eyebrow and pursed her lips. She knew exactly what Eden wanted, could practically taste the girl's desire on her tongue. Lilith forcibly pushed down the initial desire that screamed at her to push the Angel's face into the floor and punish her for the liberty she was demanding. Instead, she carried Eden to one of the sun loungers, placing her on her back with a rough hand and a heady kiss that sent Eden reeling.

Eden went to protest the position; this wasn't exactly what she had in mind. But then Lilith was stripping herself bare of her parted shirt and tiny little shorts, and all thoughts flew from her mind.

The succubus was perfection in every sense of the word. Eden had never seen anything more beautiful than those long, pale legs, the hourglass of Lilith's waist, the slight dips between her hips and upper thighs, the small tummy that rounded out the otherwise slim physique. It all made her near mad with desire, unable to think of anything except pressing her lips and tongue to every piece of offered skin.

"*Fuck,*" she whispered, her eyes devouring the form slowly crawling up her body.

"Is this what you want, Angel?" Lilith taunted, finally reaching her destination where she hovered on her knees above Eden's mouth.

Eden looked up at the glistening pink flesh above her face and licked her lips. She reached up to brush her fingers over Lilith's inner thighs, the feather light touch meant to tease and coax the demon into lowering herself onto Eden's mouth.

Lilith still wasn't entirely comfortable with the act, a hesitance that was born from a long history of dissatisfaction and loss of control, but if this was what Eden needed, then at least she knew she would not be left wanting.

Eden could feel Lilith's reluctance and began peppering sweet kisses along the demon's thighs. "After you ride my mouth, I want you to fill me in every way possible," she whispered, nearly laughing when Lilith immediately lowered herself onto her face.

Sometimes it was clear who was the succubus and who was the Angel, other times, like now, the lines grew blurry as Eden gently coaxed Lilith's own repressed desires to the surface.

Eden did not move to immediately press her tongue to Lilith's clit. She teased the outer area, running her tongue through the slick folds, enchanted by every gasp and shudder the motions pulled from the mythical being perched above her face. Lilith sank further onto her mouth, the muscles of her thighs relaxing as she became more at ease with the tentative touches.

"Pet," she breathed out, jolting when Eden's tongue briefly flicked over the hood of her clit before darting away once again.

In a bid to claim some control over the situation, Lilith bent forward to press kisses to the Angel's jeans-clad thighs. She popped the button on Eden's trousers, intending to lose herself to the sweet distraction of the Angel's cunt, only for the woman to reach down and still her hand.

"Just *feel,"* Eden stressed, begging for her to give herself over to pleasure. She pressed her thumb to Lilith's clit, moving her fingers to gently push them against the entrance to the demon's pussy.

"*Oh!*" Lilith gasped, arching her body and grinding herself down onto the teasing fingers. "Yes," she whispered, clutching at the thick thighs under her hands. Her own shook and quivered around Eden's head, threatening to drop her entire weight onto the Angel's face.

Eden suppressed a smile and gently scraped the nails of her free hand over Lilith's ass. The demon moaned and shivered, tipping her head back under the touch and bucking her hips. Lilith was like a cat, Eden had discovered. Prickly and picky, only wanting affection when it suited her. But she had managed to find a weakness or two over the last couple of months.

Flattening her tongue, Eden rubbed it against Lilith's clit as she held the demon's twitching hips in place. Her own body felt hot and wired, on the verge of combustion if Lilith so much as breathed upon her.

She thrust her fingers into the demon, answering Lilith's deep, growling moan with one of her own. As always, Eden knew that she would pay for the liberty she was taking. But fuck, it would be worth it.

Lilith couldn't believe that such a sweet creature could own such a wicked fucking mouth. How Eden hadn't fallen from grace already was a mystery to her. She rocked her hips in time with Eden's tongue, pressing down onto the fingers gently curling into her, pleas and moans tumbling from her blood-red lips.

"Right there," Lilith groaned, *"right fucking there!"*

"That's it; you taste so good," Eden praised, sucking Lilith's clit back into her mouth and flicking the tip of her tongue against the pulsing bud.

Lilith fell forward over Eden's body, barely catching herself in time before she smothered the girl below her.

Eden strained to breathe as Lilith rocked against her face, smearing arousal over her lips and chin, but even still, she continued her motions.

"Come for me," she moaned, steadily pushing Lilith over the edge with her sweet-tempered touch and gently thrusting fingers. As Lilith began shaking and bucking onto her mouth, Eden curled her fingers, dragging them over the spot deep inside of the demon that would make her see stars.

Heat unfurled throughout Lilith body, and she could no longer hold herself up as her limbs tensed and stiffened. She cried out, curses tumbling from her lips. Blistering, pulsating pleasure lingered between her legs, warming her body in ways that Hellfire never could as she came.

Eden hummed below her and continued sweeping her tongue through Lilith's cunt, eagerly drinking up the sweet ambrosia of the demon's cum.

"I'm going to butcher every one of your past lovers," Lilith gasped when she could finally do more than frantically pant for breath. "I'm the only one who should ever know the pleasure of your tongue."

Eden laughed and helped the boneless body above dismount from her face. She made a mental note to never give Lilith names, having no doubt that her lover would follow through on the threat if given the chance.

Lilith settled beside her to kiss her jaw, gently biting at the plump cheek under her fangs as she moved to claim the Angel's lips.

Eden was in for it, and she knew it.

The deadly glint in Lilith's eyes, the raking of her nails down her arms, it all told her that she was about to be well and truly fucked in every sense of the word.

Lilith ran her tongue over Eden's chest, sucking her nipples into her mouth and biting down, hard enough to pull a pained hiss and a pleasured moan from the Angel below her.

"Are you going to show me who you belong to, pretty girl?" Lilith purred, squeezing at the skin of Eden's wide hips, shocking the Angel by abruptly pulling her down the sun bed so that her ass lingered on the edge.

Lilith stepped back, resisting the urge to push her hand between her own legs as Eden spread herself to bring her knees up to her chest, baring herself and her dripping cunt for Lilith to devour. She drank in the sight of Eden's soaked lower lips. The trimmed patch of brown hair at the apex of her thighs was soft and inviting, just begging Lilith to bury her nose in it as she drank from the divine well of Eden's soul and desire.

Eden's stomach bunched and rolled under the position that left her open and vulnerable to the demon above her, and Lilith groaned as she stepped closer, ghosting a barely there touch over the back of the whimpering Angel's leg.

She lowered herself to her knees and finally unburdened her, allowing Eden to wrap her legs around her head as she swiped her tongue over her clit.

"Oh, shit!" Eden cried out, having long ago learnt not to utter the word 'God' during sex.

"Where do you want me, Angel?" Lilith teased, circling Eden's entrance with her fingers and blowing on her clit with an icy burst of magic.

Eden jerked away from the abrupt piercing cold lingering on her sensitive bundle of nerves, and almost arched off the sun bed entirely when it was immediately followed by the blistering heat of Lilith's talented mouth.

A gargled groan of disappointment left Eden's lips when Lilith pulled back, rubbing her thighs and reaching up to pinch and squeeze her breasts. The demon slapped them, loving the sight of the flesh bouncing and turning pink under her strikes.

"Use your words, pet. Or I will leave you wet and wanting, your pussy dripping for me and begging to be fucked."

They both knew it was a lie.

Lilith was far too possessive over Eden's pleasure to allow such a thing. But the dirty words, combined with the teasing touch that never quite stayed where she needed it, prompted Eden to speak.

"Anything you want, my clit, my cunt, my mouth, anything you want, just please, *fuck me*,"

Eden begged, forcing down the desperate sob that rose in her throat at the continued denial.

Lilith bit her lip to suppress the bubble of laughter that threatened to rise.

"Such dirty words for such a good girl, pet. Do you think you've earned it? Do you think your sweet little tongue satisfied me enough for me to fuck you?"

Eden frantically nodded, clawing at Lilith's shoulders as she tried to pull the woman's head back to where she so desperately needed it. Lilith stood, abandoning her place from between Eden's thighs, and the Angel almost screamed her frustration.

"Lilly pl–" Eden didn't get to finish her plea.

Lilith thrust into her, burying her magically summoned strap inside her with a single motion that made Eden's eyes roll back into her head and her mouth drop open with a guttural moan. Her back arched, curving off the sun bed at the sudden penetration.

It didn't hurt. Eden was so very wet and wanting, so helplessly eager to be used and abused that Lilith met no resistance at all. "Paradise," she rasped breathlessly at the feeling of Eden stretching around her, eagerly taking all that she was willing to give.

It was bigger now. With Eden more comfortable with penetration, she didn't shy away from the eight-inch phallus. Though, the Angel had requested one slight change.

After much embarrassment and hesitancy, Eden had asked if she could change the colour to something a little less… realistic. A request that Lilith had no problem with whatsoever, but still made the woman pay for it by taking the newly purpled appendage into her mouth.

"Fuck Lilly," Eden whimpered, wrapping her legs around the demon's waist as Lilith entwined their fingers, pinning her hands above her head.

"This is what you were made for, pet. To be fucked, used and abused."

The words only inflamed Eden's passion. Partly because they were entirely true. Sometimes she really did feel as if she were only created to take whatever torment Lilith's imagination could unleash upon her. An imagination that was truly, remarkably extensive.

"Only by you," Eden groaned, barely able to breathe through the rough roll and slapping of Lilith's hips against her own. "Only you."

Lilith gentled her kisses but not the pounding force of her thrusts, knowing that any change in rhythm would push Eden away from the impending climax glazing over her eyes.

"That's right, pet, only me. Are you going to cum for me, pretty girl?" Lilith rasped, tightening her hold on Eden's hands until her knuckles turned white as she strained to hold off her own release that was so tantalisingly close.

Eden's spasmed around her, going rigid as her mouth opened and closed, her face turning red as she gasped for breath that she could not suck in fast enough.

"Lilly," she cried out, clenching the thighs around the hips relentlessly driving into her.

"You can take it. You feel so fucking good," Lilith moaned, continuing to buck her hips and thrust into Eden through her climax.

Eden screamed as she was pushed into a second and then a third orgasm, her body becoming hypersensitive and engulfed by the heat of Lilith's passion.

"Please, *please*," she begged, not knowing if she was pleading for the demon to release her from the sweet torture, or for it to never end. But either way, Lilith just laughed and wrapped her hand around Eden's throat, cutting off her air in short bursts that made the Angel splutter and choke.

Lilith pulled the magical strap out almost to the tip and slammed forward one last time, the defined muscles in her back and legs tensing and straining as she jerked and cursed, dropping her head to Eden's chest to bury her fangs into her breast as she came.

The sunbed finally gave out beneath them, dropping them to the floor as the legs collapsed and broke under the violent motion.

Eden's vision went white, spots swimming before her eyes as the stinging pain of Lilith devouring her soul sent her careening into another earth-shattering climax that stole whatever will she had left.

Lilith felt Eden fall limp and still below her, and she smiled into the flesh between her teeth. When she'd taken her fill, she pulled back, still breathless and panting from the sheer intensity of their lovemaking. Pulling out gently, she brushed Eden's hair aside, pushing and peeling it away from her sweaty skin.

Lilith kissed the unconscious woman deeply, smearing Eden's own blood over her mouth before swiping her tongue across those sweetly pink lips, cleaning up the remnants of her feeding.

She swept Eden into her arms, carrying her back into the apartment, and she chuckled a little as the Angel's head lolled into her neck.

It was a shame; they'd made many memories on that sunbed. Perhaps one made of steel might hold up better under her strength and Eden's own growing power.

Lucifer's coin glared up at her from the bedside table, dark in its malevolent aura and calling to be reunited with the creature it hadn't been parted from in countless millennia. Lilith ignored it, curling around the unconscious form of her pet as she stroked Eden's hair.

"What have you done to me, pretty girl?" She asked aloud, her voice soft and open in the knowledge that the Angel would not hear.

Chapter 4

Eden awoke to the smell of bacon. The blankets wrapped around her were warm and comforting, almost restrictive, and she smiled as she fought to free herself from the thick cocoon Lilith had built around her.

She peeked open her eyes, her mouth watering and her stomach grumbling at the heavenly scent drifting from the kitchen. She couldn't see her clothes, and she did not yet keep any in Lilith's apartment, so Eden pulled the demon's way too small robe around her body before going in search of her lover.

"Honestly, I thought this room was mostly for show," she quipped, leaning against the doorframe and smiling bemusedly at the frustrated look on Lilith's face. So far, the only thing they'd used the kitchen for was to fuck on the table.

Lilith glared up at her, looking haggard and two seconds away from lighting the room up with hellfire. She glowered at the oven door, releasing a growl that made the hair on Eden's arm stand on end.

"The eggs aren't working," the demon seethed, her tail whipping back and forth in agitation at her perceived failure.

Eden glanced about the kitchen, taking in the equipment that hadn't been there the day before and the numerous ingredients littering the sides.

"And why, exactly, are the eggs in the oven?" She asked, restraining the giggles that threatened to burst free.

Eden shooed Lilith away and opened the oven door, coughing slightly as a thick plume of black smoke emerged. She couldn't help it; truly, she tried. Eden burst out laughing, clutching her stomach at the sight of what she presumed was supposed to be scrambled eggs on a baking tray.

Lilith grumbled and glared, taking one of the newly purchased tea towels and whipping it across Eden's butt cheeks. The stinging pain made her jump, but the situation was too ridiculously funny for her to stop laughing.

"Unless we count you, I do not eat." Lilith said defensively, "How am I supposed to know how food works?"

Still shaking with mirth, Eden cupped Lilith's cheeks, bringing the demon down into a chaste kiss. "It's sweet that you tried. But uhh, I am not eating that," she said lightly, pointing to the tray of burnt bacon. "In the thousands of years you've been alive, did you ever think about taking a cooking class?" She asked cheekily, bringing the succubus close to soften the effects of her teasing.

Lilith merely huffed, eyeing the burnt food with contempt and disgust. She ordered Eden breakfast from the restaurant down the road, watching with sharp eyes and a scowling face as the Angel rifled through the newly acquired purchases as they waited.

"What on earth is this?" Eden asked, shaking one of the boxes. The instructions looked to all be in Chinese, with not a single clue or picture on the cardboard to indicate what it might be used for.

Lilith shrugged. "I called up the kitchen appliance store on main street and ordered one of everything they had in stock," she said with a careless flick of her wrist.

Eden bit her lip, retreating to the bathroom so that she could laugh freely without further dampening Lilith's already sour mood.

Like she'd said, the demon could get a little *sensitive* when it came to the more human side of a relationship. But aside from the occasional unwelcome presence of Lucifer and the demons hellbent on killing her, life for Eden was blessedly happy.

At times, Lilith still felt more like a stalker than a girlfriend, not coming to her for days on end and only watching from the shadows, taunting her with those magically whispered words. But those moments grew few and far between as Eden began to see the woman under the monster who claimed her.

Her mind rarely drifted to her heavenly brethren, and she assumed that they held as little interest in her as she did them. An assumption that her demonic protector did not share. Lilith rarely ventured far out of fear for her continued 'ownership' over her. A term that made Eden both preen and roll her eyes, laughing indulgently at the demon's obsessive, territorial urges.

One delivery, and one very traumatised delivery boy later, Eden sat munching on a near orgasm worthy breakfast sandwich, moaning a little as the yolk popped into her mouth.

Lilith snorted, watching with a faint measure of disgust as Eden practically inhaled the food. She'd never understood the allure, but Eden held enough appetite for the both of them. Though, Lilith had to admit that she was more than fond of the deliciously curvy results.

"Do you want some?" Eden tried to tempt, waving the sandwich in front of Lilith's face.

The demon smirked. "I'll take a bite when you do," she dared, holding her wrist out in offer.

Eden baulked and pulled back with a sheepish grimace, taking a hasty bite of the sandwich in her hand. While she often enjoyed the blood play Lilith liked to indulge in, she couldn't say that she was particularly keen on the idea of drinking someone's blood.

"Are we going out?" Eden asked after finishing her late afternoon 'breakfast'. She watched, near hypnotised by the red stain Lilith was applying to her sinfully skilled lips.

The demon paused, eyeing her in the mirror and grinning, displaying the long, deadly fangs that often pierced Eden's flesh.

"I'm going hunting, and then I have some business to see to. Would you like to come and play with me?" Lilith asked conspiringly, tugging on the front of the robe that Eden had stolen from her.

It was a little small, clinging to the Angel's wide hips and not completely closing over her breasts, but Lilith adamantly refused to buy a new one. She was far too obsessed with ripping open the fabric that strained to keep her pet covered.

Eden hesitated, eyeing the stack of books and the mountain of homework she'd been neglecting. She also wasn't entirely sure what Lilith's definition of 'hunting' was.

But regardless, Eden tipped her head from side to side before nodding. She was curious to see more of the demon's world, as so far, Lilith had kept her as far away from all things supernatural as possible.

Lilith hummed and spun her around, eliciting a sharp gasp from Eden as her face was pressed against the mirror that became misted under her breath.

"I'm not so convinced," Lilith murmured into her ear, opening the situation up to a little extortion. Eden laughed and pushed the robe from her shoulders, exposing the soft rolls of her waist and the dimples above her glorious behind. Lilith drank in the sight greedily, a darkly affectionate glimmer lighting up her malevolent blue eyes as her claws grew sharp and deadly, scraping over Eden's skin hard enough to leave pink streaks over her skin.

**

Lilith watched, ever attentive but not interfering as Eden tried to fight off the demon they'd lured into the alley. Her blood burned in a possessive rage at the thought of anyone but her snuffing out that precious light. But Eden had asked that Lilith not interfere, so she waited, with impatient eyes and a snarl split across her lips, for her pet to signal that she needed help.

It was a minor level demon, barely more than a gnat under Lilith's boot. Under close supervision, the fight would be a good experience for Eden, who often didn't understand what the allure of her divine blood did to the demons swarming the city.

Eden cursed and ducked under outstretched claws, nearly tripping over in the process. In all honesty, she was doing a pretty shit job of 'hunting.'

It didn't help that the demon looked human, the only difference being the small red claws and teensy tiny little fangs that poked free of his lips.

Eden questioned if the creature really deserved the fate it was to meet at Lilith's hands when the succubus finally lost patience. He was probably just in the wrong place at the wrong time.

"Duck, pet," Lilith said, her bored tone completely contradicting her inner feelings. She picked at the purple polish on her nails, blowing the chipped paint into the air as she watched the scene with gritted teeth.

Eden was too late to heed the warning. The demon's fist connected with her cheek with a dull 'thud' that made Eden cry out in pain as she stumbled into the alley wall.

Lilith's restraint snapped.

She pushed out of the shadows, plucking the demon into the air and holding him aloft by the back of his neck like an unruly pup.

"I had him," Eden protested weakly, shaking out her wings and crossing her arms. Her face throbbed, the slight pain making her wince and raise her fingers to the upcoming bruise.

Lilith hissed as it began to bloom on the skin of Eden's cheek, and she tightened her grip around the demon's neck.

"He was wiping the floor with you, pet. Know when you're beaten and retreat," she growled, glaring at the creature in her clutches as he shook in fear, soundless pleas spewing forth from his gasping mouth.

Eden grumbled but conceded the point. He was well and truly kicking her ass. "Do you have to kill him?" She asked quietly, looking pityingly at the shaking demon in Lilith's grip. "Can't you just send him to Hell or something?"

Lilith raised an eyebrow, cutting her eyes to the squeamish woman. "I *could*," she purred, pursing her red lips. "But I won't." His life was forfeit the second he'd glanced at her pet, and Lilith felt not an ounce of pity or remorse for her merciless actions. Hellfire erupted from her claws, engulfing the creature and burning him alive with flames that licked and ate at his skin, devouring him whole.

Eden turned away, trying to block out the sickening screams, only for Lilith to tip her head back up.

"Do not shy away from it, Angel. He would've killed you, watch him burn," she tempted, running one of her claws down Eden's neck.

Eden screwed up her eyes and shook her head. "That's enough, Lilly, please," she pleaded, splaying her fingers on Lilith's shoulders, beseeching the demon to grant the creature a merciful death.

It did not matter to her that his intention had been to kill her, she could not bear to watch as he suffered.

Lilith eyed her irritably, cursing the Angel's painfully human nature. Even most 'light' supernaturals she'd encountered had more of a stomach for pain and torture than her sweet pet. She intensified the fire, leaving the demon nothing more than a wisp of smoke trailing up to the sky.

Eden swallowed thickly; she knew this was her own fault. Despite the occasional sweet gesture, Lilith wasn't kind, wasn't benevolent, or good in any way, and Eden knew that; loved it even. Especially when that teasing cruelty was directed at her.

But that didn't mean she didn't struggle to accept some facets of the woman she loved. The ruthless bloodlust and desire to slay every creature that so much as looked at her, being one of them.

Lilith wrapped her arms around Eden, pulling her to her chest with a faint rumbling purr in her throat. The Angel's distress seemed paltry and trifling to her, but she had learnt to indulge it, nonetheless. "Come, pet," she said softly. "I have something to show you." Lilith shook out her wings to take to the sky, flying over the city below that was still bustling with activity, despite the late hour.

"It's not another severed head, is it?" Eden shuddered, recalling the minotaur head Lilith had brought her on, unbelievably enough, an actual silver platter.

Lilith laughed and squeezed the Angel tighter. "I think you'll like this one," she murmured, pressing a kiss to the side of Eden's cheek.

All of her previous distress forgotten, Eden melted into the sweet motion, returning it by pressing gentle kisses to Lilith's neck and jaw as they flew.

Chapter 5

"A dive bar?" Eden asked, eyeing the dingy exterior of the club. Rubbish built up around it, overflowing from the graffitied bins. The ashtrays on the tables were stained and murky with rainwater that mixed with the sopping remains of cigarettes. Overall, it was not exactly Eden's idea of a date.

Lilith chuckled.

"It doesn't look like much, but trust me, pet, appearances can be deceiving." She said, grinning down at Eden in that wicked way of hers that told the Angel she would either really love it… or find it entirely horrifying.

"I should know better than to trust you," she said doubtfully as Lilith wrapped her arm around her waist to pull her towards the entrance.

"Yes," Lilith agreed, in that sultry way of hers. "You really should."

They slipped through the chipped, rickety old door, and Eden grunted when her limbs became heavy and slow, as if she was trying to walk underwater while held down by weights.

Lilith watched her struggle for a moment, curious to see if her growing power would be enough to fight the enchantment.

It was a tricky piece of magic. One she'd paid a High Witch handsomely for, as Lilith's magic did not extend to such intricate warding systems.

Hellfire, mental projection, soul manipulation, illusions, and transfiguration were a veritable arsenal of abilities, but sometimes a little outsourcing was well worth the hassle of dealing with lesser supernaturals.

Lilith despised witches. Scam artists and haughty, disrespectful little cunts; the lot of them. But they certainly had their uses... occasionally.

The Angel got so very close, but eventually, Lilith took pity on her struggle, grasping the girl by the back of her neck to pull her through the enchantment.

Eden gasped and her knees wobbled, threatening to tip her forward as Lilith pulled her through the unbearably heavy force.

But then she gaped.

And then gaped some more.

"Where are we?" She breathed, looking out at the club in a mixture of awe and horror.

Lilith smiled widely, winking at the Angel as she shook the illusion from her form. Small, pointed horns rose from her head and her fingers lengthened, forming into sharp claws. Her wings stretched wide and proud, alerting all that the mistress of the house had returned to her domain.

A long black tail poked free from her tight leather trousers to wrap around Eden's thigh, bringing a subtle comfort to the plump woman who suddenly looked so very nervous.

Lilith enjoyed and sometimes even sought to ripen Eden's scent with the sweet tang of fear, but it was not something her possessive nature was willing to share. Especially with her demon brethren, who eyed the Angel at her side hungrily, eager to see if she would share her spoils.

Lilith would sooner snap Eden's neck herself than allow a single one of them to lay their filthy hands on her.

"You don't live as long as me without acquiring a little blood money, pet. This is what I like to do with mine," she said carelessly, as if the sheer opulent nature of the club was little more than a trifle.

And in fact, it truly was.

Lilith imagined taking Eden to one of her more exclusive clubs, places where the Angel would follow behind her on hands and knees, a collar wrapped around the pretty throat that was forever marked with her teeth. Arousal twisted in her gut at the mere thought, and her grip on Eden tightened, eager to seek out somewhere more private to indulge in the fantasy.

Eden followed Lilith in a daze.

Her eyes darted to the shadowed figures dipping and twisting in cages mounted to the walls, running their hands down their bodies in an erotic display that was almost masturbatory.

A mammoth chandelier topped with red candles illuminated the room, twinkling with what Eden was certain were *actual fucking diamonds*. The melting wax dripped down, mimicking a constantly flowing river of blood that disappeared before hitting the grinding throng filling the dance floor.

"What is this place?" Eden squeaked, her eyes darting from face to face. This was no normal human club, she realised with a frantically pounding heart.

Demons sat at the bar, some as large as elephants, their twisting horns nearly hitting the ceiling. A feathered creature with wings instead of arms launched herself from the balcony, her taloned feet perching on the edge of a booth as she chirped and chittered to the inhabitants.

Scales, horns, tails, tentacles, wings, fangs, hooves, fur, feathers, extra arms or legs, double heads, or no head at all. You name it, someone had it. And they all turned to stare at Lilith, whose mere presence brought simultaneous feelings of terror and desire. Then their gaze shifted, uncontrollably drawn to the deliciously frightened prey at her side.

"Lilly," Eden whispered, growing increasingly alarmed at the sight of the creatures surrounding her. Regret sunk to the pit of her stomach, and she cursed her impulsive desire to immerse herself deeper in the world of the supernatural.

Lilith felt a rumbling purr begin in her chest in response to Eden's fear, and for once, she didn't fight the noise. Wrapping her wing around the Eden's body, Lilith shielded her from view as she led her up the black marble stairs to her private balcony.

Eden tucked herself close to the demon's body, holding the edge of the great leathery appendage and pulling it around her like a blanket to soothe the fear bubbling under her skin.

"It doesn't quite bend like that, pet," Lilith chided, her voice a little strained at the uncomfortable feeling of her wing muscles being stretched and bent at an awkward angle.

Eden blushed and loosened her grip with a sheepish apology. "Sorry."

"What is this place?" She asked as Lilith guided her to a plush leather couch. Instead of sitting beside her, she crawled into Lilith's lap, running her hands up to grip the small horns on the demon's head. Eden frantically strained to remind herself that Lilith wouldn't allow her to come to any harm. Not that wasn't by her own hand, at least.

"Welcome to the Devil's Dealings, pet." Lilith said proudly, gesturing to the teaming club below.
"Demons and those of neutral bloodlines are welcome, but not creatures of the light. A unicorn once wandered in here by accident. The poor thing had her mane shorn and her horn sawed off, but she left alive," she said passively, her eyes scrutinising every minute expression on Eden's face.

Eden pulled back, her eyes widening in shock. "Unicorns are real?" She blurted, almost swooning at the thought of the mythical creatures.

Lilith began scratching her nails over Eden's jeans, running her touch higher until the Angel clamped down on her fingers, trapping her hand between her thighs.

"Not in the way that you think. Adorable things, truly. They love to grant wishes for good little girls. Somehow I don't think you'd quite qualify," Lilith taunted.

She had fucked and seduced her own fair share of the creatures over the course of her long life, delighting as their silver eyes and glittering skin became mottled and streaked with red when they fell to the darkness of her touch.

"But Lilly, I'm a creature of the light," Eden fretted, her wings tensing under her skin and threatening to burst free. Would the demons swarm her if she revealed herself? Would they sever the wings from her body and mount them upon the walls with the rest of the trophies?

"You are mine," Lilith reminded her, pressing a possessive kiss to Eden's lips. "No one here would dare. While in my house, every one of them bends to my rule."

The words eased Eden's spinning mind somewhat, and she returned the kiss. As she tried to pull back, Lilith bit her bottom lip, tugging on it playfully as her touch grew soft and soothing.

Lilith hummed contentedly when Eden eventually relaxed into her body. She watched, her narrowed eyes meeting every demon and creature below, warning them with her gaze that this toy was hers, and for once, she would not share.

A small group of women slinked up the stairs, scantily clad and eager for the renowned touch of the succubus. It wasn't often that the mistress of the house graced them with her presence, and those brave enough strained to catch her eye, hoping to elevate themselves at her table.

The group of women lingered at the top, awaiting Lilith's approval before daring to enter her space.

"Do you like them, pet?" Lilith murmured against Eden's ear, flicking her tongue over the outer shell. The touch brought shivers to Eden's body, and it took a moment before she comprehended who the demon was referring to.

She looked up at the awaiting entourage, her eyes growing impossibly wide at the sight before her.

Oh, Christ.

One of the women lowered herself to her knees, crawling closer and swaying her hips as she approached. Her skin was speckled with purple scales, and long, pointed ears twitched on the side of her head as she grinned, revealing a sharp mouth tipped with fangs.

"What is she?" Eden blurted, only to wince and wonder if it was rude to ask.

The creature giggled, lingering at Lilith's feet. Her eyes ventured to Eden as she stretched her arms above her head, arching her back in invitation. She was quite familiar with the succubus' games and didn't take the warning look as seriously as her companions.

"She's…" Eden trailed off, unsure of how she felt at the sight of the creature. Hot, for one. Wanting and aching at the sight of the woman lifting her black hair and tipping back her head, displaying her long swan-like neck.

But then the creature looked to Lilith, and a furious burst of jealousy burned in her chest, curdling her building arousal and turning it sour.

"Do you like her?" Lilith asked again as she squeezed the extra flesh on Eden's tummy, kneading it with her fingers. "Mermaids are such desperately needy creatures."

The succubus' tone sounded more like she was asking if Eden liked a piece of meat or a cow at market, rather than an actual person. Or at least... sort of person.

"Like her for what?" Eden asked cautiously, not entirely sure of where the demon was going with this. Did Lilith want to invite the woman to their bed? If so, she would find herself on the end of a very cold shoulder.

Lilith hissed out a laugh and bounced her knee, bobbing Eden up and down. "As if I would permit such a thing," She rumbled possessively.

Lilith fully understood the impression that Eden was getting, and while it was amusing, the thought of the mermaid's hands on *her* Angel, caressing and kneading the curves that belonged solely to her, nearly tempted her to rip the head from the creature's body then and there.

And yes, she was well aware of her hypocrisy.

"Would you like her to dance for us?" Lilith asked patiently, suppressing a smug smile at the ever-tightening tick in Eden's jaw.

She was so very easy to tease.

"Just dance?" Eden asked cautiously, glancing down at the disappointed mermaid.

Lilith hummed her agreement, pointing to the small table before them, and the mermaid hurriedly rushed to obey.

Eden hesitated, flicking her eyes between the erotically dancing form and the demon watching her with such blazing intensity. "This is a test," she huffed, crossing her arms and turning away from the mermaid at the realisation. "If I watch, you're going to light her on fire."

Lilith tipped back her head and laughed, her long hair cascading down the back of the sofa. "Oh Angel, I would rip the scales from her body," She confirmed coldly, waving her hand to dismiss the group of women from her space entirely.

The mermaid atop of the table squeaked in fear, frantically rushing to pull on the clothing she'd been peeling from her body. She stumbled down the stairs, closely followed by the rest as they sought to escape Lilith's vicious gaze.

"That was mean," Eden scolded lightly, biting her lip to stop from laughing. It was a harmless prank, one that hadn't ended with someone being decapitated, so Eden didn't feel too bad about joining in with Lilith's mirth.

"Hmm, yes, but it got the message across. Did you expect flowers and rainbows from me, pet? If so, I'm afraid you're going to be sorely disappointed," Lilith said, gesturing impatiently to the shaking waiter whose eyes never once left the wobbling tray in his hands.

In truth, no, Eden didn't expect those things at all. She knew exactly who Lilith was. Knew the things the demon would do for pleasure, what she did for duty, for spite, for rage or jealousy.

The darkening tease in Lilith's eyes, as well as the violence in her actions and words, were equivalent to jewels and flowers in Eden's mind. To her, the brutal gestures were just as romantic, even if she occasionally went a little too far.

The shaking server placed a martini on the table for the mistress of the house before hesitantly adding a second drink beside it, quickly retreating into the shadows without so much as making eye contact with the duo.

Eden looked at the bright pink, glittery cocktail curiously, but before she could reach for it, Lilith tightened her hold to pluck it up instead. The demon lifted the glass to her mouth, watching with smouldering eyes as she wrapped her pretty pink lips around the straw.

Eden hummed and sucked the drink down, never once breaking her gaze away from the liquid heat building in Lilith's icy orbs. It was sweet, mildly alcoholic, with a slightly bitter tang that lingered on the tip of her tongue.

"Thank you," she whispered bashfully, a blush rising on her cheeks under the intense scrutiny of the succubus. It was ridiculous really, how such an action could make her feel silly and shy, especially when all of the other depraved things Lilith demanded from her barely raised any response at all.

Lilith hummed and smiled, tucking the Angel into the crook of her neck and turning her attention to the figure slowly sauntering up the stairs.

He wore no shirt, only a red blazer that parted to reveal the small silver bars poking through his nipples. He radiated poise and elegance, his entire being dripping with sexuality that could nearly rival her own.

Lilith greeted the newcomer with a sneer and a curled finger, summoning him into her space.

"The lady of the house returns. How very disappointing. I thought for sure you'd finally succumbed to old age and crawled up in a corner to die like some mangy old cat," he said, stretching out onto the sofa opposite them.

Eden abruptly sat up, sucking in a sharp breath as her eyes darted between Lilith and the interloper so carelessly insulting her. Not even she dared to speak to Lilith with such casual disregard for her power.

Lilith cut the man a baleful glare, but only grunted, rolling her eyes with a tolerant expression on her sharp face.

"Eden dearest, meet Erik, who one day will be no more than a scorch mark under my boot once his usefulness has expired," she said boredly, gesturing to the flamboyant man with a flick of her fingers.

Erik threw his whole body back onto the sofa, clutching his heart as if the words had mortally wounded him.

"She adores me really," he reassured, throwing a cheeky wink in the Angel's direction.

Eden held her tongue. She doubted it.

"Don't flatter yourself, I tolerate you." Lilith shot back.

"Well then, I truly *am* honoured," he said with mock breathlessness. "How many people can say they are tolerated by the Mother of Monsters?"

"A tolerance that wavers with every word from your mouth," Lilith snapped.

Eden expected Erik to cower and shrink back from Lilith's dark tone, but to her surprise, he only twirled a finger through his shoulder-length blonde hair, fluttering his eyelashes up at the demon as he giggled.

"Don't pay the prickly old lady any notice, Angel. She's just jealous of my rakishly good looks and endless charm," he boasted, toasting his drink towards Eden.

Despite herself, Eden laughed, deciding then and there that she liked him. Anyone with a tough enough clit to tease Lilith and live to tell the tale was someone she definitely wanted to be friends with.

"It's nice to meet you," she said, leaning forward and holding her hand out for him to shake. Lilith grumbled but allowed the touch, even if her lips curled and her eyes narrowed at the sight of someone touching her property.

"Oh, she's adorable," Erik gushed, throwing Lilith a scorching look that was all play and no substance. "May I pet her?" He asked mockingly, as if Eden were a puppy on the end of a leash.

"By all means," Lilith said amicably, and Eden nearly fell off of the demon's lap in surprise. "You have such pretty hands. They'd look marvellous hung around your head like a necklace."

Erik clapped said hands and laughed, clicking his fingers at the server lingering in the shadows. "Did you like your drink, doveling? My own creation, I made it just for you." He cooed, turning towards her and gesturing to the glittery pink drink in her hands.

Lilith sighed impatiently at the chatter.

Picking Eden up, she carefully placed the Angel back onto the sofa, shooting Erik a warning look all the while. "Since you're here, I have some business to attend to. Watch over her, will you?"

It was framed like a question, but Lilith walked away without waiting for an answer, and

Eden watched her go with a slowly deepening expression of distress.

"Crotchety old bitch, isn't she? If I had a quid for every time she threatened to kill me, I'd be almost as rich as her," Erik said. He jumped up from his place opposite her, flopping down into Lilith's vacated seat with an exaggerated flair and a lively grin.

Despite her amusement, Eden tensed, shuffling away in an effort to put some space between her and the unknown demon.

"So, the drink?" He asked again.

"It's delicious, thank you," she responded shyly. She didn't feel as brave without the commanding presence of her demon.

"Wonderful. I wasn't sure what kind of effect pixie dust would have on an Angel, but I figured 'her royal highness' wouldn't let you drink something that might hurt you."

Eden glanced down at the swirling pink glitter in her drink, quickly putting it back on the table without taking another sip.

Nope.

Demons, yes. Mermaids, yes. Unicorns, she was struggling with a little. But drinking tinker-bell, her favourite cartoon character as a kid, just hit the limit.

"Why do you call her that?" Eden asked, tucking her legs under her body. Her eyes automatically ran over the area below, searching for her demonic protector in the crowd.

Erik hesitated; if Lilith hadn't explained her position, then he wasn't about to get himself into hot water by doing so. He was a tease, an ever-present annoyance tugging on his mistress' tail, but he wasn't suicidal.

"Well, she is the lady of the house." He lied, gesturing to the opulent room that somehow managed to be both extravagant and trashy at exactly the same time.

Liar.

Eden jolted at the sound of her own voice ringing through her ears, alerting her to the demon's less than honest words. For a moment, she thought it was Lilith; speaking to her in that weird way of hers that no one else could hear. But it felt different, lighter, in comparison to the usual heaviness of Lilith's dark magic.

Eden narrowed her eyes on the demon, but he only shot her a charming smile, leaning in close as he spoke.

"So precious, the entire supernatural world is just *dying* to know, how are you retaining your grace? Some of them literally, because Mummy dearest is hunting down almost every demon who doesn't seek permission before entering her territory."

Eden bit her lip and ignored the clenching in her gut at the word 'mummy.' Well, that's something to never bring up or unpick, literally *ever*. She had no doubt that Lilith would revel in the potential kink, but she felt a flush of embarrassment at the mere thought.

But judging by the look Erik was sending her, the way his painted red lips curled at the end and his icy blue eyes gleamed cheekily, Eden held no doubt that he knew.

"I don't know what you mean," she responded quickly.

"Come now; don't be coy. Angels have fallen for far less than fucking a demon. I mean, look at poor Belial; he fell simply for failing to live up to the hypocritical standards of heaven. Bit rude though, dubbing him Belial the worthless just because Daddy thought he was a disappointment."

"Leave her be, Erik." Lilith snapped, reappearing at the top of the stairs.

Erik flinched this time, sensing that he was getting dangerously close to the edge of Lilith's very limited patience. He winked at Eden, leaning in to whisper into her ear. "If you ever want to come out on the town and have a little fun without the cougar, give me a shout," he said, his teasing grin losing some of its inherent malice as he met the Angel's wide brown eyes.

Poor thing, he thought, pitying the creature trapped in Lilith's deadly web of desire.

Lilith flashed her fangs, and realising that his presence was no longer quite so tolerated, Erik blew Eden a kiss as he jumped to his feet. He brushed the creases out of his suit and flicked his hair behind his ear, and as he passed, he brushed his body against the succubus, pressing a lingering kiss to her cheek.

"Sorry, mummy," he teased, shooting the Angel a pointed glance.

Eden groaned internally, mentally pleading for the plush leather sofa to swallow her whole as she glared at the back of his stupidly perfect head.

Lilith pursed her lips and rolled her eyes at the overstep, but she let it slide in exchange for settling herself back at Eden's side. "Take no notice of the little rat. He thinks that just because I fucked his mother, it grants him some sort of leeway," she said, pulling Eden back into her lap.

As always, the few pieces of paperwork marked for her attention were needless and excessive, something that any half-decent manager should've been able to handle. She certainly paid him enough to do so, and she'd expressed her irritation in a grossly disproportionate manner by stapling his endlessly flapping lips together.

Eden blushed at the unexpectedly vulgar words, and she glared at Erik's retreating form with renewed vigour.

Her ire was unfair; it wasn't exactly his fault. But even still, he was extraordinarily beautiful for a man, and Eden held no doubt that his mother would be just as stunning. Something that twisted her chest into little jealous knots.

"I like him, he's a little pushy. But he seems sincere." She said, adjusting her body to place her legs on either side of Lilith's so that she was straddling the woman. "Is it rude to ask someone what they are?"

"Is it rude to ask a human where they are from or what their culture is?" Lilith countered, rubbing her hands along the thick thighs spread atop of her.

"Depends on the context," Eden replied immediately.

Lilith smiled and nodded. "The premise is the same. But to answer your question, Erik is an incubus. Half, to be precise, though it's more dominant than the elf blood in his veins."

Eden flicked her eyes between Lilith and the man enthusiastically dancing with what looked like a living statue. She swallowed hard when she noticed the similarities between Erik's glowing blue eyes and those of the woman below her.

Surely not... right?

"Would you like to dance?" Lilith asked suddenly, breaking Eden from her thoughts. She shifted on Lilith's lap, looking over the railing of the balcony to the dance floor below.

"Down there?" She asked doubtfully, eyeing the thick, grinding throng of creatures. With the way they moved, Eden was half certain it was just one great big orgy.

Lilith laughed, keeping Eden cradled in her arms as she stood, and the Angel gasped in her hold as they launched into the air. They glided around the chandelier dripping with blood, and Eden squealed in delight as they spun quickly to the music.

She reached up to wrap her arms around Lilith's neck, stroking the sides of her face as she stood perched on the demon's feet. Their eyes locked. Eden's gentle brown gaze becoming dark with desire while Lilith's icy orbs lightened with affection as they danced above the watching crowd below.

"Buying me fancy gifts, romantic dates to your den of iniquity, keep this up, and they might just revoke your ticket to Hell," Eden teased.

Lilith shot her a vicious grin. "Oh darling, I earn that ticket every single day simply by feasting on your flesh," she whispered, her voice brimming with dark promise. Lilith ran her hands over Eden's sides, forcing the Angel's upper body back so that she was dipped and splayed before the being holding her with such deceptive gentleness.

A woman in a slinky black dress started singing below, her voice low and seductive as she rolled her hips to the song. Nearly nude waiters ventured through the crowd, shaking their assets and encouraging patrons to slip tips into their sheer undergarments. In the corner of the room, a half-giant kneeled before a leprechaun, his head bobbing up and down in the creature's lap.

But despite it all, Eden could only see Lilith. Her heart was bursting with happiness as she was held in the arms of the monster who claimed her.

"I love you," she whispered, with such gentle longing.

Lilith's wings jerked, barely catching them before they became engulfed in the writhing throng below.

Eden watched anxiously as the woman's luminescent eyes blinked rapidly and her mouth opened and closed several times. Eventually, she took pity on her, cupping Lilith's tense jaw in her hands.

"You don't have to say it, and I won't say it again if you don't want me to," Eden said softly, trying to push down the fierce pang of pain that tore in her heart.

It was unjustified, and a little silly of her. Lilith had never hidden her motivation, never concealed the fact that she viewed Eden as property or as a toy to be played with.

One she cherished and cared for, sure.

But loved? Eden didn't expect it from her, wasn't pushing for it or demanding it; she merely wanted to express her own inner feelings.

"I-" Lilith started, licking her lips and looking incredibly uncomfortable.

Fuck, what should she say?

'I love you too, maybe?' A sarcastic inner voice taunted her, sounding infuriatingly similar to Lucy's usual jaunty tone.

"Really, Lilith, it's okay. I understand that you don't feel the same, I just wanted you to know." Eden insisted quietly, leaning in to kiss the prone demon.

"*I love you.*"

"*I love you.*"

"*I love you.*"

The words taunted Lilith, mocking her and her inability to process them. She returned them to the balcony, running a hand through her black hair, tugging on the ends as her mind raced under the weight of unwanted memories.

"Lilith?" Eden questioned, not used to seeing the demon lose her composure in such a way. Her stomach twisted with nerves, and Eden started to get the sinking feeling that she may have made a terrible mistake.

Lilith seemed to be even paler than usual, a feat that she didn't think was possible. "It's okay, really, I-"

Lilith cut Eden off. "I treasure you," she blurted out. She brought the Angel close, her purple tipped claws ever so slightly digging into the Angel's supple skin in her distraction.

Eden smiled and tipped her head back to gaze up at the demon. "I know," she said earnestly, nodding her head, trying to reassure the woman that she really, truly did understand.

Eden guided Lilith to sit back on the leather couch, climbing onto her lap as she splayed her fingers over the demon's chest. She lingered just above Lilith's breasts, pressing her hand to the frantically pounding heart beneath Lilith's skin, before reaching up to cup her cheeks.

"Can you make us invisible?" She asked, glancing down at the demons who couldn't help but watch.

Lilith glared down at the crowd and clicked her fingers, weaving an illusion to protect their privacy. The balcony became engulfed in an impenetrable wall of darkness that no demon could see through, cloaking their forms under a veil of shadow. Several huffed in frustration, squinting at the force and trying to see the scene they could hear happening above.

"I *know*," Eden whispered devoutly, staring down at Lilith like she was the only thing that mattered, the only thing that existed even.

Eden popped the button on her jeans and tugged off her trousers. She watched, wanton and breathless, as Lilith did the same, the tight leather peeling from the demon's legs like a second skin. "The strap," she whispered against Lilith's jaw, grinding down onto the demon clutching at the bare skin of her thighs.

Lilith moaned as Eden rolled her hips and pushed herself up, only to sink back down and repeat the action over and over. It was slow and sensual, gentle and passionate in a way that rarely came to them.

She gripped Eden's waist tight, watching the bouncing of her large breasts and stomach as the Angel rode her to pleasure. Lilith drank in the sight, loving the way the body above her moved, entirely lost in the sway of the Angel's hips and the parting of her pretty pink lips as she bared her throat, arched her back, and moaned for all to hear.

"Just like that," she praised, her voice barely more than a gasping moan as Eden's tight pussy clenched around her.

Eden reached up to grip Lilith's horns, using them as leverage to pull herself up as her legs began to shake under the strain of her movements. Their breaths mingled as she remained barely a centimetre from the demon's lips, the air becoming thick and almost unbearably hot, threatening to overwhelm and suffocate them in the intensity of the near connection.

When Eden brought Lilith's mouth to her neck so that she could feed, the demon did not sink her fangs into the soft flesh. Instead, she kissed it, sucking it into her mouth and encouraging Eden to continue her motions as she tasted the sweat and desire gathering on the Angel's skin.

"Lilly!" Eden cried out as she came, clamping down around the strap inside of her. It twitched, and Lilith groaned, burying her face into Eden's breasts as she came inside of her, painting the Angel's insides with her scent and claim.

"Fuck, I never thought I'd love that as much as I do," Eden gasped, resting her forehead against Lilith's. It had been odd at first; strange to feel and even stranger to see, especially after the strap had been turned purple, but she'd quickly come to enjoy and even anticipate the feeling of Lilith's cum inside of her.

Once again, she thanked the heavens that pregnancy wasn't something she had to worry about.

The demon chuckled and kissed her. "Well, far be it for me to deny you something that makes you happy," she murmured against Eden's mouth, turning the laughing Angel onto her back and beginning their passion anew.

Chapter 6

Admittedly, the club wasn't exactly Eden's favourite place in the world, mostly due to the ever-watchful eyes of the demons around them.

But even still, she gasped and clapped along with the rest of the patrons when Lilith clicked her fingers and an aerial show of very nearly nude performers took to the air, launching themselves from hoops and performing daring tricks.

The difference in power between them was startling, jarring even, for Eden to realise. Not just in sheer strength or magic, but again, in *the stupid shit money could buy.* Eden knew that Lilith was loaded, but this was something else.

So, when Lilith tried to present her with a small silver card one day, Eden's face twisted in irritation at the, admittedly sweet, but also completely unnecessary gesture.

"I don't need your money, Lilith," she sighed, turning her eyes to the living room ceiling with an exasperated huff.

"You were *literally* just complaining about the cost of the 'shit your university tries to pass off as food,'" Lilith said dryly, using her fingers to form quotation marks.

Eden stubbornly set her jaw and tried to give the card back, but the demon just snorted and turned back to her book.

"Besides," Lilith said absently, licking her finger to turn the page. "I have more money than I know what to do with. You could put a few million on there a day and I'd barely notice."

Eden's mouth dropped open and she gaped. "You know just because I said the 'L' word and you didn't, doesn't mean you have to throw your money at me to make it all better," she said sharply, her own sense of pride rising at the casual dismissal in Lilith's voice.

"I love you."

"I love you."

"I love you."

The words taunted Lilith, whose face tightened at the memory. "Just take the card and buy yourself something skimpy so I can peel it off of you with my teeth," she said, forcibly pushing the unwelcome reminder away.

Eden plopped down onto the sofa beside her, tugging on the demon's tail with wide eyes and a spluttering mouth. "Why don't you use your money for something better? Donate it to charity, hell, build a hospital!" She exclaimed. "If you'd barely notice a few million a day, imagine the good you could do in the world."

Lilith raised an eyebrow and looked to her pointedly. "Demon," she reminded, gesturing to herself with a purple-tipped fingernail. "Doing good isn't exactly my forte, pet. In fact, it's rather contrary to, oh, you know, *only my entire existence,"* Lilith said sarcastically.

She intentionally failed to mention all of the women's shelters she already sponsored, as well as the frequent donations she made to various LGBTQ+ groups and the odd surgery she funded.

She had a reputation to uphold, after all.

Eden opened her mouth to argue, but as she did, Lilith swiped the card from her fingers, sticking it in her mouth with a sly smirk.

Like she was a god- damned ATM machine.

After a brief moment of bewilderment, Eden spat the card, crossing her arms over her chest with a victorious grin on her face as it landed in the pages of Lilith's book.

The demon pursed her lips, slowly retrieved the card, and closed her book with a sharp snap. She reached out, tangling her hand in

Eden's wavy brown hair to yank the young woman close.

Eden hissed at the mild grip, even as her eyes became lidded and heavy with lust. It didn't hurt, but the show of power was definitely arousing. She could already feel an uncomfortable ache simmering in her core, building her desire and leaving her uncomfortably wet.

"Lilly," she tried, only for the demon to place the card between her lips once more.

Lilith brushed her lips over Eden's plump cheeks, opening her mouth to scrape her fangs down her flesh. "If you want to be a brat, save it for the bedroom. Otherwise, take the card. Use it; don't use it. It's your decision. But do not tell me that there is anything better for me to spend my money on than *you*, because there isn't."

Eden moaned and tipped her head back, welcoming the slight sting brushing over her skin.

"Now, are you going to be a good girl?" Lilith murmured.

Eden let loose a gargled choke but was unable to speak around the credit card between her lips.

"What was that?" The demon taunted, pushing it deeper into her mouth.

Eden gagged, and Lilith laughed. She pulled it free, watching with a vicious expression as the Angel coughed and sucked in a breath.

"That was a little unnecessary," Eden grumbled as Lilith ran a soothing hand through her hair, rubbing away the slight sting of her grip.

"Yes," Lilith agreed with a cat like gleam in her eyes, "but it was oh so very enjoyable."

Eden laughed as Lilith snapped her fangs close to her face. Sometimes, she wondered if there was something wrong with her to find such depraved, almost abusive actions arousing. But then she'd look up at the cruel face of her sweet demon, and she knew she wouldn't have it any other way.

Lilith pulled Eden down so that her head rested in her lap, scratching her nails over the Angel's scalp as she reopened her book. Predictably, Eden lasted a whole five minutes before opening her pretty mouth once again, much to Lilith's vexation.

"Have you ever been to pride?" She asked quietly as she basked in the affection Lilith was bestowing upon her.

"I joined the first Liberation March in New York in the seventies, but not since then," Lilith replied absentmindedly, flicking to the next page. The book was one she'd read a hundred times before, but she was a sucker for a good classic. Modern fiction was also a guilty pleasure of hers that she indulged in every once in a while, much to Eden's amusement.

Eden peeked up at her.

Sometimes she forgot that Lilith was a creature who'd existed since almost the dawn of time. She sat up, looking at her hopefully. "Will you come with me to London at the end of the month?" She asked excitedly, gently tugging on the end of Lilith's tail with an insistent motion.

The demon looked down at her with exasperation and frustration, once again abandoning the book in her hand. Eden was almost chronically chatty, always asking questions about her life and experiences. And while cute, the fact that it was hindering her ability to get lost in a good book was getting on Lilith's last fucking nerve.

"And what will I get out of it?" She asked slyly. She had every intention of saying yes, but the opportunity for extortion was just too tempting.

"Me, covered in glitter, wearing a teensy tiny bikini and tiny little, short shorts," Eden said bluntly, winking at the demon before her.

"And is it your intention for me to murder everyone there?" Lilith asked, eyeing Eden's abundant breasts and trying to imagine the outfit in question.

The Angel laughed, cupping her hand over her mouth to whisper into Lilith's ear.

"Sold."

Eden rolled her eyes and giggled. "Yeah, I thought so," she said dryly.

Lilith's returning smile suddenly dropped.

"What is it?" Eden asked.

"I nearly forgot. I've been summoned to Hell for the summer solstice," she said, wincing internally as Eden's face grew tight.

"Summoned by them?" The Angel asked quietly, taking Lilith's forked tail back into her hands and running her fingers over the leathery appendage.

"They are the only one who could." Lilith replied honestly, for once not understating the position she held in Hell's domain.

"Can't they just leave us alone?" Eden said tightly.

Lilith sighed and turned to face her fully. "Lucy is like a child who doesn't like to share their toys. They also happen to be the second most powerful creature in existence. If I do not go to them, the consequences could be... *unpleasant,*" she said, with a slight curling of her lips.

Eden stewed for a moment, letting out a long, irritated sigh. "Will you be back in time to come with me to London?" She asked hopefully. She couldn't wait to show the succubus a little bit of the mortal world. As far as she could tell, Lilith was a creature of habit; rarely immersing herself in the modern world unless she needed to feed. Something that wasn't necessary with Eden around.

Lilith smiled and nodded her head. "I'll make sure of it," she promised.

As jealous as the Devil may be, there was only so much time that Lucy could, or would, hold her in Hell. And Lilith was the mistress of getting under someone's skin.

"Now, as much as I enjoy your tongue, do you think you could hold it so I can finish my book?" She asked flatly, waving said book in her face.

Eden swallowed the smile that threatened to twitch on her lips and lowered her head back to the succubus' lap. For an infamous demon from the depths of Hell, Lilith was such a nerd.

Chapter 7

The days passed quickly, their almost mundane bliss coming to an end when it came time for Lilith to leave.

Eden ground her teeth, swallowing her protests as the succubus pressed Lucifer's coin into her hand. "Why are you giving me this?" She asked, glowering down at the little black coin. It was ancient, having existed as long as the friendship between Lilith and Lucifer, and it didn't like being in the hands of an Angel one bit. The horns on its face darkened and pulsed, and Eden quickly stuffed the coin into her pocket to escape the malevolent aura.

"I will not be able to speak into your mind while I'm in Hell, pet. The coin is Lucifer's gateway to earth; they will be able to hear it if you call for help." Lilith said, focusing on the ties running up the long sleeves of her dress. It was archaic and wholly outdated, but it was undeniable that the sweeping black and red medieval gown suited the demon.

"And you trust them to do so?" Eden asked sharply, her own doubts rising to the surface, as well as her tears.

'Don't go.'

'Don't leave me,' she wanted to beg.

But it would not endear her to the demon who often struggled with such blatant displays of emotion. Nor would Eden lower herself to do so.

"I trust that they will protect their own interests," Lilith admitted. "As much as they despise your presence at my side, they would not do anything to endanger or break the treaty. A sinful world intact is far more profitable than a destroyed one."

Eden ducked and nodded her head, wrapping her arms around herself to try and hold off the wobbling lip that threatened to reveal her inner turmoil. Lilith tutted, curling her fingers around Eden's jaw, forcing her head up as she ran her thumb over the Angel's lower lip.

"When I return, I want you naked, on your knees with your legs spread and your ass in the air," she rumbled, and Eden very nearly jumped to obey then and there, just to stall the woman for a moment longer.

"Be safe," she whispered instead.

The shadows of the room grew tall and imposing, snaking around Lilith and tugging her in, swirling to form a portal of darkness. "I will be," the demon said softly, blowing her a kiss as she stepped into the portal.

Lie.

"Wait!" Eden yelled, jerking forward to pull Lilith back into the light. But it was too late; the demon was already gone, and the shadows had already stilled.

Eden pulled out the coin in her pocket, glaring down at the offending item hatefully. She went to throw it, but instead, she lifted it to her lips. "If you hurt her, I will find some way to destroy you. I don't care how long it takes."

The coin heated to an unbearable temperature in her grip, and Eden hissed as a jolt of pain shot lightning up her arm. She cried out, dropping the coin to the floor. It lay there, completely still and unassuming, but Eden somehow got the sense that it was laughing at her.

Maxx slinked out of the bedroom with a loud yowl falling from his skeletal maw. His tail beat against the floor, and he hissed at the pulsing coin. Eden sniffled, and as was his duty as her protector, he stretched up to dig his skeletal claws into the Angel's thigh, demanding that she pick him up immediately so that he could bring her comfort.

"Thanks, buddy," Eden whispered, pressing a kiss to the end of his furless snout. Her fingers slipped between the bones of his ribs as she clutched him close, taking solace in the creature as his undead body began vibrating with purrs.

Maxx's eyeless sockets darted around the room, sweeping for any danger to his charge. This woman was his mistress's chosen mate. He had a duty to fulfil and swore that no harm would come to the Angel weeping into his rigid, bony body.

* * *

Lilith appeared before the entrance to Hell. The gates rose up, blackened and gleaming in the firelight that danced across the sky above like a blazing aurora. Hell itself seemed to grow warmer, welcoming the first demon home as the realm echoed the glee of its master at Lilith's return.

At the gates, a line of souls stood gormless and half formed in a never-ending queue that stretched into the infinite wasteland beyond the city of darkness. Some blinked and reached out to her, instinctively seeking the warmth of her power to fight against the biting chill of death that nipped at their heels.

A little girl in a bloodied pink dress clutching a small stuffed rabbit clung to the bottom of Lilith's dress, and her stomach turned at the sight.

"I can do nothing for you, little one." She lied, but the blank little eyes staring up at her never once wavered in their attention. The child reached her arms up to Lilith, pleading for her comfort and care, but the demon hastily turned on her heel, abandoning her to her fate even though her deadened heart pounded in her chest to do so.

Children die every day, she told herself.

Babies, mothers, innocents.

Lilith had long since given up on trying to blanket the souls in her mercy. It was cruel and unfair, even by her standards. The tortured souls bound for the depths of Hell, doomed to wonder the sphere of the dead, did not all deserve their fate. But the rules were set long before her time, and a sin so little as a lie could damn even a child to Hell if they died without repentance.

The gates opened a crack, and Lilith felt her illusion shatter under the force of Hell's draw.

Her horns lengthened, more twisted here than on the mortal plane; her wings grew sharp, tipped with deadly spines at the end; and her eyes could've rivalled a celestial's glow in their power.

Where usually only her canine teeth were tipped with fangs, now, every one grew sharp and pointed, threatening to slice her lips to ribbons if she forgot their presence.

The great City of Darkness opened up before her, overwhelming in its opulence and horror. Even the drainpipes were decorative and scaled, the mouths opening up to resemble a snake. Demons, imps, malevolent spirits, and ghouls widened their eyes at the sight of The Queen of the Damned. They parted automatically, quickly vacating from her path as they watched in awe and jealousy as Lucifer's favourite ascended through the endless rings of the city.

The landscape shifted and changed, warping and moving buildings according to the moods of the Prince or Duke that presided over it. All of whom answered to the King of Hell.

Those in the lower rings cried out and begged her to bring them too, to elevate them in power and seat them before a golden chalice.

But Lilith was far more swayed by the little girl at the gates, and if her heart was cold enough to leave her behind, then the demons surrounding her held no chance.

A dragon nesting atop a black cathedral curled its neck to watch the commotion below, licking it's lips in desire at the sight of the regal succubus. When she passed, he turned his attention back to his dozens of wives, roaring in desire as they shrieked under his lusty attentions.

Finally, the Devil's inner sanctum opened up. The gates immediately parted at Lilith's touch, the crackling torches growing fierce in the intensity of their fire. Lilith climbed the hundreds of steps, knowing that it would be unwise to fly and risk insulting her master. The way Hell reacted to her presence clued her in to Lucy's jubilant mood, but it was probably best not to draw their ire if she wished to return to Eden on time.

"Hello, Cerbie," she cooed at the hulking beast before her. He barked, a sound and force that would've brought a lesser demon to their knees. Three heads curled around her form, fighting for her touch and affection as they snarled and growled at one another.

"Hush now, my babies," Lilith murmured, taking the middle head into her hands and pressing a kiss to his forehead. While not one of her own personal creations, Lilith had rescued the seemingly vicious creature from the fighting pits in the lower rings.

As a puppy, Cerbie's small stature had made him excellent bait, but Lilith was drawn to the uncommonly gentle soul behind the three-headed monstrosity and had plucked him from his bloody fate. Now, he was a veritable giant, easily twice her height, and truly magnificent to behold.

Cerbie whined when she released him to make her way up the polished steps. "I will take you to earth for a walk soon, my love," she promised, wiggling her fingers in parting to the creature. She blew him a kiss, softening her goodbye as he huffed and laid his heads back on his paws.

The doors opened for her, the women who held them giggling and following close behind as she traversed the grand hallways.

Lilith didn't so much as glance at them.

In comparison to Eden, they were nothing. They were small and dainty, holding none of the lush, womanly curves of her pet. And while she was known to regularly indulge in the hospitality Lucy offered, Lilith was resolute in her decision to remain loyal to her sweet pet.

Scenes of history and myth lay carved into the walls, illuminated by candles and life-like in their form.

Above the doors to the throne room, Lilith's own carving stood tall and sensual, her hair trailing over her shoulders to curl around her bare breasts as she arched up to the sky. Demons and humans cowered at her feet, their eyes and mouths wide in terror as they gazed upon her beauty.

A small smile quirked on her lips, and despite her irritation at their behaviour of late, Lilith laughed at the sight of her dearest friend bouncing excitedly before the throne.

Lucifer's face was no longer concealed by shadow and mist, and a large, beaming smile split their beautiful lips. Even after all these millennia, they never settled on a face or body, constantly shifting and in motion to match their mood or whim. But Lilith always knew; could always sense her friend and master, no matter the face they wore.

The court stood to the side, bitter and forgotten in the presence of their king's favourite. They seethed and hissed, falling into reluctant bows and muttering scalding words meant to degrade and lower her. But no matter their thoughts, none were willing to challenge the succubus, not when doing so would lead to their demise at Lucifer's hand.

"Hell's most beautiful flower, how we have missed your presence," Lucy breathed as they twirled Lilith, her dress swishing and flaring around her ankles.

Lilith gazed up at them, flattening her hand to their cheek. "My friend," she greeted joyously, dropping into a deep curtsey, and the court's jealousy grew even fiercer at the familiar title the succubus was permitted to use.

Lucy took her hand, kissed it, and guided Lilith up the steps of the dais. "Come, my wife. Join me."

Chapter 8

Lucifer brought Lilith to the throne, gesturing for her to perch beside them on the great chair. They flicked their fingers at the gathered demons, banishing them from their presence and back to their respective domains.

"Flawless, as always," Lucy praised, trailing their fingers over her jaw.

Lilith sat uneasy at the touch, but she pushed down the voice that told her she was betraying her Angel by allowing it. "You toy with them," she said, her eyes gliding over the now empty court.

Rumours of their *intimate* relationship were abound in Hell, and no one liked to stroke them more than Lucy themself, who used the misinformation to protect Lilith from the few beings capable of challenging her.

"Are we not married?" Lucifer asked innocently, fluttering their eyelashes as they lifted a jewel-encrusted goblet to their lips.

"In name only, I suppose we are," Lilith conceded with a laugh, chinking her own glass against theirs.

"I have missed you," they said, for once pushing aside their play to take her hand in their own.

"As I have you, my friend," she murmured. "But this silly feud you wage against my pet must cease."

Lucifer rumbled and growled, their face, no longer shrouded by shadow, twisted in petulance and irritation.

"Let us not sully the night with such talk. I have prepared a grand celebration for your return," they proclaimed, pulling Lilith up and holding her close as they spun her in excitement.

"Lucy," Lilith said warningly, putting her foot down on the topic. The Devil growled and bared their pointed teeth threateningly, an action that Lilith mimicked to push the seriousness of her request.

"You cannot fault my frustration, Lilith," they said sharply, guiding her from the throne room.

"I can and I will," Lilith retorted bluntly, finally relaxing into the platonic touch at her waist.

Satan narrowed their eyes on her for a moment, before sighing and shaking their head. "I miss our fun," they admitted.

"As do I, but that doesn't mean you can keep sending poltergeists to haunt her dorm. I've had to expel three in the last month alone. For fucks sake, Lucy, the last one dyed a girl's hair *orange* while she slept," Lilith said, muffling her own mirth at the ridiculously childish prank.

Lucifer opened their mouth to speak, but Lilith cut them off. "Don't even try to deny it, I know it was you. No one else would be quite so petty."

Lucy grinned, poking a finger into Lilith's side. "I had no intention of denying it, dearest wife. I merely wanted to play with your new toy, just like I did with the thousands of others you've kept over the millennia," they said slyly.

"This one's different, Lucy, and you know it. I won't share her," Lilith warned.

Lucifer held up a fist, halting the slow parting of the doors to the banquet room. "And I won't share you," they said, their ever-shifting face stilling in a moment of intense sincerity that momentarily threw Lilith off.

The doors began to open again under Lilith's silence and presumed compliance. She snapped her fingers, and they slammed shut once more. While telekinesis was not a skill she possessed, Hell responded eagerly to her commands, closing the doors with a sharp bang that echoed through the castle.

Inside, the demonic nobles of the court whispered and gossiped at the sight, straining to try and hear the presumed scandal.

"I am not a possession," Lilith hissed. "I am your friend, your confidante, and occasionally, your *babysitter.* You have no right to feel jealous over who I fuck."

Lucy huffed and eyed her in amusement. "How hypocritical, dearest, especially considering the way you treat your own pet. Not to mention the fact that you mounted the head of the last demon who attempted to take your place upon the parapet."

"Yes, well, at least it's on brand for me. From you, it's just tiresome," Lilith shot back.

Their eyes locked, waging a silent battle that, by all rights, Lucifer should win. But despite their difference in power and station, the game was never quite so clearcut. The tension mounted, neither of them willing to be the first to concede to the other.

And then, as one, they both burst out laughing.

"Come, Lilly, let us greet our *ever so adoring* subjects," Lucy said sarcastically, holding up a hand in offer.

Lilith shot them an amused look and took it into her own. "And would you like to wager tonight?" She asked, running her eyes over the now silent court.

They watched, entirely cowed under the protective glare of Lucifer as they led Lilith to her seat at the high table.

Lucy clapped their hands, and every attending demon rushed to their place. Without the rank to claim a seat in the Devil's Hall, lesser nobles lingered on the fringes, plotting and scheming their rise to power.

"I think... eighty-six," Lucy said, their eyes surveying the demons below. Only Lilith sat with them at the High table, as no other was worthy of a position at their side. It was not a matter of power, for there were indeed creatures of Hell capable of defeating the succubus. Rather, it was a question of taste, and Lucy held little tolerance for many outside of the woman at their side.

"So few? And here I thought this was a celebration," Lilith taunted, watching shrewdly as a tiny little imp of a woman filled her plate.

The meat itself was a little dubious. Not that she ate it anyway, but Lilith had long since learnt not to ask what it was after the great Kraken debacle in 1962, when one of the nobles realised he was eating a relative.

Cue an uprising from the demon lords of the depths. Not her finest moment. But the battle was fun, and Lucy's startled face when she displayed them the head of the man parading himself as 'the sea god' was more than satisfying.

Lucifer raised an eyebrow, awaiting Lilith's response. She pursed her lips and eyed those in attendance.

Someone had been stupid enough to place Alastor next to Crowley for one, which was never a good combination. The idiots could never quite work out if they were fighting or fucking.

The few mermaids in attendance were already baring their fangs at the frightened cecaelia, who cowered and hissed, waving their tentacles and wrapping the appendages around themselves defensively. Poor things.

The hellhounds and the humanoid werewolves were the first to add to the body count, snarling and fighting over the scraps of meat being thrown from the table by the laughing nobles who watched them.

And most amusingly of all, Mikte, one of her own personal creations, whom she'd forgotten to give a sense of self-preservation, was already flirting horrendously with one of the pampered daughters of the eight Princes. And the Prince's ever tightening grip on his spear was just begging for trouble.

"One hundred and… thirty-two," Lilith eventually replied, shaking Lucifer's hand to seal the bet.

"Excellent," they said, clapping their hands for what they assumed would be an easy victory. Even for a night of the darkest revelry, it was rare that the death toll exceeded a hundred.

Lilith gave a small, affectionate smile, but eyed the food on her plate in distaste. "You know that I do not eat," she reminded them for the millionth time. It wasn't that she couldn't; she just didn't particularly enjoy it.

Lucy continued to shovel their own food into their mouth, gesturing wordlessly to a sweet little demon lingering at the edges of the table. "Don't you worry," they said flirtatiously. "I'm sure there's plenty here that can fulfil even your vivacious appetite."

Lilith forcibly turned her eyes up to the ceiling, refusing to even glance at the approaching woman who looked at her with such a painful mix of hesitancy, fear, and arousal.

Lilith shooed the girl away, picking up her goblet instead. While all sex was enjoyable to her, she much preferred her partners a little less terrified. And lately, there was only one capturing her attention.

In comparison to the divine essence of Eden's soul, all others would taste like ash on her tongue.

"You will need to be strong for the challenge, Lilly," the Devil warned, their face turning tight with irritation and a slight bit of worry at the denial of their offering. "Perhaps you would like something a little plumper? Or even a shapeshifter, and you can mould her into your precious little pet," they said a little spitefully.

Lilith ignored the sour tone, running her nails up Lucy's arm to soothe the Devil's wounded pride at the rejection of their gift.

"Hmm, yes, the challenge," she prompted, "Why don't you tell me about that?"

She turned her face to her master, brushing her hand through their ever-shifting hair to fix the slight imperfections that stuck out from their head.

Lucifer huffed, knowing full well the game that Lilith was playing and the distraction she was trying to pull over their eyes. "Careful now, all work and no play makes Lilith very boring company," they warned.

Lilith smirked behind her glass. As if they would dismiss her. But even still. "Very well, dearest, let us play," she crowed, like a mother would to a particularly demanding infant.

Chapter 9

Lucy and Lilith spun around the dance floor, laughing at the carnage surrounding them. They twirled her, faster and faster, until she threatened to topple into their arms, and the room became no more than a blur.

A chime sounded, signifying the appearance of the coming dawn. Something that was barely acknowledged in Hell except for the slightest lightening of the blazing sky above. Demons swayed and stumbled around them. Nobles snoozed at their tables, not daring to retreat to their domains until their King dismissed them. The few able to keep up with the revelry continued to drink and gorge themselves on the pleasures offered by the celebration, be it violence or flesh.

"One hundred and nine, I do believe we've reached a stalemate, dearest. Whatever shall we do?" Lucy goaded, gesturing to the broken bodies of the partygoers surrounding them.

Lilith grinned deviously, running her tongue over her fangs, and as Lucifer spun her across the dance floor once again, she snapped the neck of a Cyclops who was getting a little too 'familiar' with a frightened, dainty little shadow elf.

"That's cheating," Lucy mock growled, even as their eyes danced with merriment. All knew the dangers of attending such an event. Those who survived would be elevated in power and pride, a worthwhile bet for many of the demons in Hell.

"But of course, dearest. Did you expect anything less?" She teased, straightening the lapel of their ancient suit with a playful tug.

Due to their much longer lifespans, the supernatural world progressed far more slowly than the mortal one. Even those living on Earth usually lingered a decade or two behind when it came to fashion. Lilith herself had several staff on hand to make sure she didn't fall behind the times, as she had little patience for the ever-shifting trends.

"I expected no less than perfection, and as always, you did not fail to deliver," They murmured, bringing Lilith into their side as they finally vacated the ballroom.

Lucifer did not acknowledge the demons still present and living, but all breathed a sigh of relief as the King and Queen of Hell finally departed.

Under the eyes of the thralls who didn't dare judge, they half stumbled and swayed down the hall, clinging to each other to remain upright in their inebriated state. Lilith snorted as she listened to Lucy recount a highly dramatic, and likely over-exaggerated, account of a High Witch who tried to slip them a love potion. An action that had ultimately resulted in the Witch being thrown to the ravenous pits of Hellfire that bubbled beneath the palace.

"Ever the gentle-them," Lilith said, curtseying through a choking round of laughter. "Thank you for my escort." She patted their cheek affectionately and went to enter her chambers, only for Lucifer to still her hand.

"You are my most treasured friend," they murmured, and Lilith was immediately transported back to the hastily blurted words she'd spoken to Eden.

"I know," she said softly, leaning in to brush a kiss against their cheek. "As you are mine."

***

'Really?' Lilith thought with a doubtful quirking of her eyebrows. She was sat upon a smaller black throne on the dais, just below

Lucy. Her chair was placed diagonally, so that she could gaze upon the room as well as up at her master.

Satan's court was in full attendance for the challenge; they jostled and pushed to the front in a frantic throng of horns, hooves, tentacles, wings, and tails. The already gigantic throne room had shifted, mimicking the great colosseums of ancient times with high stands and ashy, charcoal pillars that even she had to admit was impressive.

Lilith and Lucy spoke without words. The slightest twitching of their lips or the tightening of their eyes was enough to almost have a full conversation.

'What a joke, I can't believe you called me down here for this crock of shit,' Lilith's face read. Lucy just shrugged and wiggled their fingers at her, blowing her a kiss that she caught with a roll of her eyes and an indulgent hand.

A hulking creature stepped out of the crowd, her face full of eager challenge, her body straining and tensing with bulging muscles that rippled across her form. At twelve feet tall, she would tower over Lilith, and the axe in her hand was bigger than the succubus herself.

Lilith's eyes raked over the newcomer, and her lips tightened in displeasure. Fighting a Nephilim, the half human bastard children of the ancient fallen Angels, would be no easy feat. The challenger looked straight at Lilith, knowing that this was Satan's chosen, and laughed.

"Pretty giiirls don't belong on the battlefi-" the Nephilim started to drawl, only to be cut off by Lilith.

"As lawless as Hell can be, there is something to be said for etiquette in these occasions. You have not defeated me, so you will first address the King of Hell with their rightful fucking respect before you even *think* to utter another word," she said sharply, her eyes glowing with the malevolence and power of the countless souls she'd devoured.

Lucy laughed, mock swooning on their throne as they winked at her. "Oh, Lilly, you sure do know how to treat a Devil right," they said, their face splitting in amusement despite the slight trickle of unease crawling down their back.

Lilith crossed her legs, and many in attendance could not help but lower their eyes to the tall slit that threatened to bare all. The allure of the succubus was undeniable, and the tales of her conquests, both in and out of the bedroom, were legendary.

The Nephilim blinked back her shock and then smirked. "I have not defeated you *yet*, Satan's bitch," She mocked, turning her attention to the Devil and offering an insulting impression of a bow.

"My liege," she growled, and Lilith matched the sound at the sheer audacity of the creature's disrespect.

"I, Xeziel, challenge the throne on behalf of my benefactor, who, as is their right, will remain anonymous until the time comes for them to ascend the throne of the damned," Xeziel declared pompously.

Lilith scoffed and leaned back into her throne. "Victory or not, Hell would not tolerate a coward on the throne," she sneered, her fangs fully on display as she grinned. "But very well, let us get on with this farce so that I may return to earth and continue my book. State your terms."

Many laughed at the disparaging remark, and the Nephilim's face grew tight in fury and embarrassment at the casual dismissal of her challenge.

"No Hellfire. No magic," she spat, glaring down at the succubus and daring her to agree.

"I accept your terms," Lilith said calmly, picking at her purple- tipped claws.

"I *reject* those terms," Lucifer immediately snapped, snarling down at their champion for agreeing to such a foolish course of action.

The Nephilim laughed and heaved her mighty axe up, settling it over the back of her shoulders.

Lilith seethed internally and met Lucy's furiously shifting eyes. "You insult me, my master," she said through gritted teeth, her sharpened wings tensing and unfurling under her anger. "You summoned me here to fight, do not humiliate me before the court with your denial."

Lucifer's eyes darted between the eagerly awaiting crowd, Xeziel, and finally, back to Lilith. "Lilly," they growled lowly, but when she only continued the steady eye contact, they heaved a long-suffering sigh and slumped back onto their throne.

Lucy waved a hand for the challenge to continue, an action that seemed careless and uninterested to many, but Lilith could tell by the unnatural stillness of their form that they were worried.

"Have a little faith, lover," she purred, her blood red lips curling around the words before falling into a sharp, fang filled smile.

Lilith slowly descended the stairs of the dais, her hips swaying and the slit parting with every step, and all creatures in attendance felt their mouths grow dry at the sultry movements. There were few in existence who could resist the magnetic allure of a succubus, for her mere presence all but assured satisfaction.

Lilith stood before the Nephilim, cupping her palm around her cheek as she spoke in an imitation of concern. "Can you see your desecration, darling? All of the depraved, deliciously wicked things the horde is going to do to your body once you sink into the sand with my claws buried in your neck."

Xeziel ground her teeth and twirled her axe. "You're all talk; everyone knows the only good succubus is one who's on her fucking knees," she taunted, taking a step closer as the crowd whispered and jeered at the derogatory comment.

Lilith laughed, the sound sending shivers down the Nephilim's spine. "Oh, I won't argue that it's what I do best, but personally, I much prefer to mount my conquests from behind," she sneered.

Lilith bit her tongue to keep from laughing as Lucifer groaned, their eyes slipping closed in disbelief at the bold statement. Though truly, they shouldn't be surprised. Lilith liked tugging on their tail as much as they enjoyed tugging on hers, but the bloody rumours that statement was going to spark would never cease.

"Choose your weapon, Devil's whore," Xeziel spat, her hulking form pacing up and down the arena, kicking up the black sand below.

Lilith stretched lazily, her arms reaching up to the sky and pushing her breasts together, and this time, not even the Nephilim could resist the urge to look. She slinked closer and met the challenger's furious gaze with a smouldering pout.

"I choose… me," she whispered, spinning wide and slicing a line down the Nephilim's chest with her tipped wings.

Xeziel roared her outrage and stumbled back, swinging her axe high and slamming it into the ground where Lilith had stood a mere breath before. The giant pulled back, aiming to cut her in two with a punishing blow, but Lilith was already on the move. She tipped back, her upper body almost folding in half to avoid the swing that sliced through the air above her nose.

Despite all of her casual bravado, there was a very real possibility that the Nephilim could beat her. In sheer size and strength alone, Lilith was outmatched. Without her magic, she would need to be extremely careful not to allow Xeziel to gain the upper hand.

But Nephilim weren't exactly known for their smarts or their ability to stay focused during battle. In the war of old, the beastly creatures were well known for sending as many allies to their graves as they did enemies.

"Is that all you've got, sweet thing? You must've been the runt of the litter. No wonder Daddy abandoned you to slum it in Hell's bottom ring with the rest of the bottom feeders," Lilith taunted as she took to the air, Xeziel's swinging axe never far behind. She flew rings around the half Angel, prompting it to spin faster and faster in an effort to catch her as she raked her claws down her back and arms.

The Nephilim turned suddenly, launching herself in the opposite direction, and Lilith wasn't fast enough to avoid the coming blow. "*Fuck-*" she cried as the back of the axe slammed into her body, sending her flying through the arena, where she landed with an almighty crash in the stands.

The demons around her ran for cover, knowing that the Nephilim wouldn't hesitate to bring the battle to the sidelines. Nor was it against the rules.

Lilith wheezed in a breath, smacking her head onto the floor at the feeling of her splintered ribs piercing her lungs. She coughed, and a shower of black blood erupted from her lips, trickling down her chin and neck to pool in her cleavage.

The Nephilim laughed, stalking forward with cocky movements and a sure swagger. "And here I was, under the impression you had a little more fight in you. But what more can I expect from a little slut whose only purpose was to lay on her back and spread her legs?" Xeziel said spitefully, lifting her arms up to the crowd to tempt them into joining her showboating.

Lilith's broken ribs popped back into place, and she let out a pained hiss at the sensation of her bones refitting themselves under her skin. She snarled up at the Nephilim through a mouthful of blood, and forced herself to her knees as she approached.

Lucifer tightened their grip on their throne, the usual playful malevolence burning from their eyes. Their chest heaved in fury, and the entirety of Hell's domain echoed the response just as violently at the sight of its favourite demon struggling to rise to her knees.

Lilith was being quite literal when she said that Hell would not allow a coward upon the throne. Few understood that the underworld itself was more than just a plane of existence, rather, it was one massive consciousness, one entity that they all resided within.

Towers toppled in the great City of Darkness, demons fled as fire rained from the sky, and all shrieked at the vicious trembling of the ground below as the underworld roared its fury.

The Nephilim charged forward, raising their axe to render Lilith as little more than a red stain on the floor.

"Lilly!" Lucifer cried, their eyes wide and their words sharp. But they could not interfere, to do so would forfeit the throne and put them both to death.

Lilith rolled to the side, using the sharpened tips of her wings to slice through the back of the giant's knees. Xeziel screamed as her legs buckled, frantically swinging her axe in an attempt to keep the succubus away while she healed.

Lilith launched herself into the air, flapping her wings and spinning to avoid the Nephilim's axe as she lunged for her throat, finally sinking her fangs into the challenger's skin.

Xeziel's soul tasted rotten and filthy on her tongue in comparison to Eden, whose very essence called to be devoured and taken. Rather odd, considering their shared ancestry, but souls often reflected the vessel containing them. The viler the host, the more wretched the soul would taste.

When Lilith pulled back, she spat a mouthful of muscle and flesh onto the floor, watching with satisfaction as Xeziel's blood bubbled and spurted from the open wound on her neck.

The Nephilim fell forward from her knees, dropping the mighty axe and landing with a great thud that pulled up a massive cloud of black sand and dust.

The nobles didn't dare clap. Not yet. They waited, eagerly watching as Lucifer gazed down at their champion in contemplation.

Lilith's chest heaved in exertion, and her still mending bones cried out their protest, but even still, she kneeled before her friend. "Shall I fetch you a trophy, my liege?" She asked, gesturing to the fallen body of her foe. The crowd roared and stomped their feet when Lucifer finally held out a hand, lifting their thumb to the fiery sky to signify their approval at the victory.

"No. Throw her body to the crowd," they said disdainfully, calling for Lilith to once more join them upon the dais.

The demonic nobles howled and jeered, descending on Xeziel's body like a pack of ravenous wolves as they fought to take their own trophy from the occasion.

"Eight point two," Lucifer glowered, reaching out to press their hand against her still creaking bones. Lilith sighed with relief as they instantly healed, rolling her blood-stained body this way and that to stretch out the muscles.

"I deserved a nine for the trash talk alone," she tutted, hooking her arm through Lucy's elbow as they guided her from the room and into the seemingly endless maze of hallways.

"It *was* a nine point four until you got half the bones in your body smashed to pieces. How could you be so reckless as to agree to fight without your magic?" They snarled, grabbing Lilith by the neck and backing her into the wall.

"I would not have failed you," she snapped, wincing as their grip tightened in fury. The black stone wall behind her began to crack under the force, and Lilith wheezed a breath through her blood-stained lips.

"It was not myself I feared for! If Xeziel was victorious, I could've simply chosen another champion, and then another and another until she was defeated. But there is no other *you!*" They yelled, their worry and rage blinding them to the fact that they were hurting her.

As her panic and anger grew under the hold, Lilith could only hold herself back for so long out of respect. "Lucy," she tried to plead, but she did not have the breath to bring the words to life. With great reluctance, Lilith summoned Hellfire to her fingers, raking her claws down the Devil's face.

They released her with a pained shout under the blow, and Lilith gasped for breath as she slumped onto the floor. They went to strike her for the insolence, but when she flinched, when she looked up at them with such wide, hurt eyes, they jerked back, yanking at their constantly shifting hair.

Lucifer picked Lilith up from the floor, pulling the succubus into their chest with desperate hands. "Forgive me, my friend; I forgot myself," they whispered into her hair.

Lilith swallowed the urge to smack them again and sagged into the hold. But when Lucy went to heal the bruise darkening around her neck, she harshly slapped their hand away.

"You will endure the mark being on my skin, just as I did your anger," she said sharply, knowing that this would be more of a punishment to them than any other.

Lucifer swallowed hard and nodded their head as they carried their champion through the wide, arching halls, intent on finding somewhere for her to rest. They watched over her, gently wiping the blood and gore from her form, but not even the Devil dared to anger her further by healing the mottled black and blue bruise marring her neck.

As Lilith slept, Lucy leaned down to press the slightest kiss against her cheek. "I'm so sorry… for everything," they whispered. But despite the apology, they were set on their course.

***

"Must you leave so soon, dearest?" Lucy asked as they escorted her to the gates of hell. They had tried to stall her, pulling her into games and banquets. Even taking her down to the lower rings to watch some of the more uncivilised entertainment held there. Considering the general debauchery that Hell was drenched in, 'uncivilised' was truly an understatement.

Unfortunately, their momentary lapse of control left them with little leverage in their game, so other than a mild protest, Lucifer could not deny Lilith's decision to leave.

"My pet awaits me. While I have been at ease knowing she holds your coin, I do not wish to further test the protections I left by prolonging my absence." Lilith said bluntly, for once not skirting around the mention of Eden to soften their ire.

Her stay in Hell had only lasted three local days, but she would have no way of knowing how much time had passed on earth until her return.

It was how she'd managed to miss the entire sixteenth century. Lucy had needled her into joining them on a truly unsurpassed bender that resulted in Hell almost being evacuated and every demon who could escaping to earth. The resulting fallout in the mortal realm had created many of the myths and legends the mortals knew today, sparking what would lead to decades of witch trials and an uncountable number of atrocities.

Lilith had already forgiven Lucy for the strike. It wasn't the first time in their longstanding friendship that they'd hurt each other in a fit of temper, and she doubted it would be the last, but for now, it granted her the upper hand. The bruise still lingered though, as even her advanced healing struggled under a blow struck by the King of Hell, who's mere touch held its own magic.

Lucy let out a long sigh of discontent and playfully poked at her healed ribs. "What is it the mortals are saying nowadays? Whipped?" They asked, forcing a lighter tone into their voice.

Lilith sniffed and gave them a teasing shove. "Oh, my my, keeping up with the times, are we?

Remind me to find a way to connect you to the internet; perhaps you can torment someone else for a change," she said, muffling her laughter at the mental image of the Devil trolling through social media. It would be a disaster, but it was so very tempting.

Lilith greeted Lucy with a mocking bow as they held open the gate, but as she passed through, her smile faded and grew strained.

"Might I request a trophy of my own before I leave?" She asked quietly, running her glowing blue eyes over the souls queuing to enter the depths of hell.

Lucifer followed her gaze and shrugged their shoulders. "I have a feeling you would take it regardless of my permission, so for friendship's sake, you may," they said indifferently. "Just don't get caught."

Lilith smiled and dropped into a real curtsey this time, one worthy of her Master. She collected her trophy, smiling a little at the swirling white mist cupped between her palms. She would need to provide it with a new vessel, but Eden loved children, and Lilith couldn't think of a better souvenir to give to the Angel.

"Lilly," Lucifer called to her as the shadows of Hell lengthened and swirled into a portal. "I'm sorry."

Lilith went to ask what for, only to gasp as Lucy lifted their hand, pushing her through the shadows and back into the mortal world. She all but fell through the portal, still half turned with a question lingering on the tip of her tongue.

Dramatic little shit, she thought, righting herself with a shake of her head and a roll of her eyes.

"Honey, I'm home!" She yelled sarcastically, her usually malevolent face bright with excitement. She wouldn't admit it to Lucifer, but she was starving, and her first call would be to sink her fangs into Eden's divine cunt. Lilith licked her lips, imagining all of the depraved, wicked things she was going to do to her Angel.

"Pet?" She called again, only to pause at the sight of Lucifer's coin sitting innocently on her pillow. She snatched it into her hand, rolling it over her fingers as she frowned.

"Eden," Lilith said sharply, her voice echoing and amplified with a touch of magic, commanding the girl to come forward. A trace of unease lingered under her skin, knotting around her heart, and Lilith rushed from the bedroom.

"No," she breathed, looking out at the destroyed apartment. It looked like the after scene in one of those action movies Eden liked, with upturned furniture, broken glass, and scorch marks smattering the room.

Disbelief and fury raged within her at the small pile of shattered bones that crunched beneath her boots, but when Lilith spotted a pale, dainty little hand sticking out from under the bookshelf, her heart all but stopped.

Lilith threw the shelf aside, unmindful of the fact that she was adding to the destruction surrounding her. "Erik, Erik!" She said urgently, slapping the man's face none too gently. "Fuck, come on, you little rat, wake up. EDEN!" Lilith screamed, searching the remains for any sign of the Angel.

But there were none, and the incubus in her arms stared up at her with glazed, dead eyes no longer illuminated with power.

Chapter 10

Eden flipped through her textbook in a poor attempt at studying, before losing interest and throwing the book aside. Maxx glanced up at her from his place on her lap, stretching his paws forward to knead at her tummy.

Eden smiled at the adorable monstrosity keeping her company and ran her fingers over his exposed bones. "I don't suppose you know when she'll be back, do you?" she asked, feeling slightly ridiculous for talking to a cat. But then again, Lilith's car had literally kicked her out for calling it old-fashioned, so her attempt seemed justified.

Maxx opened his mouth, and Eden leaned in excitedly, only for the creature to let out a bone-cracking yawn. "Probably for the best since you never stop meowing anyway," she said, with a mixture of disappointment and relief.

A knock sounded, and Eden jumped, startling Maxx who hissed up at her grumpily. She set the cat on the sofa and slowly made her way to the door.

No one ever knocked.

In fact, Eden was half certain that no one else even lived in the building at all, despite the fact that it was basically a skyscraper.

She peered through the peephole and almost jumped at the sight of a giant, glowing blue eye staring back at her. Heart racing, Eden yanked open the door with a beaming smile on her lips to launch herself at the figure behind. But when she came face to face with a stylish red suit and blonde hair instead of her love, Eden's smile immediately dropped.

"Erik," she squeaked, blinking at the demon in surprise and backing away to tuck herself behind the door.

"Well, don't look too happy to see me." He said in mock offence, winking at her as he forced his way into the stately apartment.

Eden grunted as she was pushed back with the door, and a deep frown lingered on her lips. "Lilith isn't too fond of having people in her uhh… den? I think she called it." She said nervously, gesturing to the still-open door for him to leave.

Erik snorted and glanced about the room curiously, running his eyes over the opulent furnishings and the various antiques on display.

"Funny, I expected more of a leather and dungeon vibe over a stuffy museum," he said, settling down next to Maxx and poking his fingers through the cat's ribs.

The undead creature flicked his eyes between Eden and Erik, only to sigh and curl back up to go to sleep. Eden relaxed marginally at the response, or rather, the lack of one. She had no doubt that Maxx would sense it if she were in danger of being murdered by the demon.

"Lilith's not here at the moment; would you like to leave a message? I'm sure she'll be back soon." she said unsurely, wincing when she realised that she'd revealed the fact that her protector was no longer present.

"What are you, her fucking secretary?" Erik asked bluntly, a devilish gleam in his icy blue eyes. When only Eden shuffled from side to side, glancing between him and the door once more, he sighed and rolled his eyes. "I know she's in Hell, sweetness. The King likes to make a spectacle of Lilith's visits, just to put the other nobles in their place, and news travels surprisingly fast between realms," he said, twirling a finger through his golden hair.

"Then why are you here?" Eden asked warily.

"Oh, baby girl, don't look so frightened. Surely Mummy mentioned that she hired a babysitter to come and play with you?" He teased, gesturing for her to sit beside him on the sofa with a playful pat.

Eden groaned at the word 'mummy' and threw herself onto the cushion beside him. "I can see why Lilith threatens to kill you every two seconds," she said, her face relaxing into a small smile as he wiggled his fingers in her direction.

"She's been threatening that for the past sixty years. I understand that an old cat can't learn new tricks, but really, she could at least get a little creative," he said, shaking his head with such exaggerated disappointment that Eden couldn't help but laugh.

Maxx picked his head up to glower at the pair for interrupting his nap, *again.* He gave a rumbling growl, stretched out his limbs, and slinked off to find a more suitable spot.

"The saying is 'an old dog can't learn new tricks," the Angel chuckled, wondering if all demons were quite so out of touch with modern sayings. Lilith got close, but every so often,

Eden would have to bite her tongue and swallow her laughter as the woman said something so completely wrong, and with such complete confidence.

Erik just smirked and leaned in close. "Are you calling her a bitch, little dove? Because I wholeheartedly agree," he whispered mischievously.

"You *are* trouble," Eden stated, shaking her head as she giggled.

"Only in the most deliciously wicked way, I assure you," he responded, poking his tongue into his cheek and bobbing the skin in and out in a suggestive manner.

Eden snorted out a laugh and eyed the impish man, focusing on the glowing blue of his iris.

"Are you hers?" She blurted out, her mouth running ahead of her brain and spilling the question that was playing through her mind. Eden blushed but didn't retract the words. The curiosity was killing her, and she'd be the first to admit that she was too chicken shit to ask Lilith.

Erik didn't look offended, or even surprised, by the question. He shrugged, shifting to make himself more comfortable.

"Lilith is as old as dirt. You can't be terribly surprised that she has a few bastards here or there. They don't call her 'The Mother of Monsters' for nothing, you know," he said dismissively, as if he wasn't turning Eden's world upside down.

She swallowed thickly, trying to process the new information. "But umm… how?"

Erik guffawed, flicking back his hair as he shot her a mock pitying look. "Oh, dove, the birds and the bees can get a bit complicated when it comes to the supernatural. It's not always sperm meets egg, and creature inheritance can be a bit tricky. Think of her more as… my blood donor, if you will. A liberty my mother paid for with her life."

Blinking back her surprise, Eden recoiled as if struck and stared at him in horror. "And you're just… okay with that?" She asked in disbelief.

As someone who'd never known her birth mother, and was then bounced around foster homes until the age of ten, Eden struggled to understand Erik's blasé attitude. Her foster mother, while hesitantly loving and attentive, never truly made much of an effort to understand Eden. And when she came out as gay... well, that was a whole other matter entirely.

It was one of the reasons Eden had yet to introduce Lilith to her. That, and she wasn't entirely confident that Lilith wouldn't murder the woman for making some offhanded comment about her sexuality. So, for Erik to be so flippant about the death of his own mother at Lilith's hands, it hit a little close to home.

The incubus frowned, eyeing her up and down in a way that made Eden itch. "She's not human, precious. You can't judge her by mortal standards, and for your own sanity, nor should you," he said, and Eden was startled by the sudden serious nature of his voice.

"I'm not," she tried to protest. If anyone knew not to judge Lilith by human standards, it was her.

Erik just snorted and eyed her shrewdly. "My mother broke the law, one set by the universe itself, when she created me. Lilith's actions were a mercy compared to what the dark court wanted to do to her."

"Because she didn't ask permission?" Eden asked, a little confused and not at all understanding how making a baby could be punishable by death.

"Because she created me full stop. Lilith exists under the Devil's protection, and I exist under hers, but the only reason I still live at all is because my blood is split with my elven mother's. Succubi are *supposed* to be outlawed by Heaven, Hell, and Earthly powers. What my mother did could've sparked another war."

"Because Lilith is so powerful?" Eden asked doubtfully. Her love was strong, but not unbeatable, as was proven in the battle against the Knight of Hell.

Erik shook his head, opening and closing his mouth several times as he deliberated what to say. "Because succubi are the only creatures capable of bringing a soul back to the mortal plane, which goes against the fundamental laws of life, death, and creation," he admitted eventually, watching Eden closely to see if she understood the gravity of his statement.

Eden rolled the words over her mind, not fully grasping what the incubus was saying. "That doesn't seem so bad," she said, looking to the demon for further explanation.

Erik pursed his beautiful red lips and couldn't hold in the inherent impatience that started to leak into his tone. Giving an Angel a history lesson wasn't exactly his idea of fun.

Getting up, he snatched a bottle of wine from the rack and pulled the cork free with a quick burst of formless magic.

"Lilith's creation, and subsequent curse, is universally regarded by all as a great big cosmic cockup. The only other being capable of breaking the universal law, is God himself. Lilith kind of exists in an odd state between... diplomatic immunity and constant persecution, from all sides," Erik stressed, emphasising his words with his hands through a thick gulp of wine.

Eden's eyes widened. "Oh," she whispered.

Maxx slinked back into the room, and Eden watched the undead cat's lifelike motions. She'd assumed that the creature was some sort of imitation or animation of a once beloved pet, but now, she realised that there was no mistaking the genuine soul lingering in the skeletal form.

How creepy.

Adorable, but yeah, creepy, nonetheless.

"Sooo, are we just going to sit here and... wait?" Erik asked when the thoughtful silence of the room became too much for him.

Eden made a small noise of amusement at the fidgeting demon and cocked her head. "What did you have in mind?" She asked hesitantly, becoming increasingly nervous as his face split into a mischievous smile.

After much persuasion, teasing, and a healthy amount of bullying, Erik pushed Eden out into the street. "Oh Darlin, if I swung that way, I'd be almost tempted by your 'heavenly assets," he teased, throwing his arm around Eden's shoulder as she laughed.

"I don't think I'm supposed to leave the apartment," she said, hesitantly allowing him to tug her into the taxi. Erik shot her a sideways glance, one that almost screamed, 'Seriously?'

"What are you, her prisoner?" He asked, already knowing the answer. Eden may welcome Lilith's dark attentions, but he wasn't stupid enough to think that she would just be able to walk away if she changed her mind. Erik only hoped that Eden realised it too, before she ended up chained to the succubus' bed for all eternity.

Eden crossed her arms over her cleavage and grinned. "A willing prisoner is still a prisoner. I just happen to like the view from my gilded cage," she snarked, and Erik laughed heartily at the response.

"Well, I assure you, Doveling, you'll like the view just as much from where we're going," he purred, and Eden swallowed hard at the glimpse of Lilith in Erik's devious eyes.

"You are your mother's son," Eden said flatly, studiously keeping her eyes away from the dancing figures winding around the poles onstage. She was certain that if she looked, Lilith would know and probably rise up from the underworld just to punish her. Which then tempted her to do just that. The thought alone was enough to make her thighs clench and her stomach twist in desire.

Erik gasped and glared at her, completely aghast. "How very dare you. Steal a damsel from the dragon's tower, show her a good time, and this is the thanks I get?"

Eden smothered her laughter and accepted the shot he offered with a playful wink. "I mean, sixty years old, you're hardly young and spritely anymore. Are you sure you can keep up?" She teased, fluttering her eyelashes up at the flamboyant man who narrowed his eyes at the challenge.

"Drink." He mock commanded, folding up the sleeves of his immaculate red suit as he lined the bar before her with an array of colourful shots. "The first one to the middle gets to pick our entertainment."

Obviously, Erik won. But Eden found herself having fun anyway, despite the fact that his idea of entertainment was having nearly nude men dancing and shaking their 'stuff' in her face. Honestly, the poor dancers looked almost as traumatised as she did, and Eden burst into giggles when she realised that she was probably the only pair of tits in the building.

Erik stuffed a fifty-pound note into the dancer's tiny little G-string and tried to coax Eden into doing the same.

"I literally can't think of a single thing I'd like to do less!" She burst between gasps of laughter, handing the relieved man the note instead. "And what is it with demons and money? Do you sell your soul and boom, unlimited cash to burn?" She asked, knocking back another glittery shot. Eden wasn't just tipsy; she was well on her way to being full-blown shitfaced. "And if so, where do I sign up? Because the rent for the dorm room I barely even use is *killing* me."

"Oh sweetness, it's hilarious that you think your soul is still yours to bargain with," he chuckled. "Besides, what about that snazzy new card your sugar mama had me set up? I mean, maybe don't buy a whole ass country, but she wouldn't even blink about an island."

Eden snorted and crossed her arms, looking at him irritably. "You're as bad as she is. I don't want her money. I want her – I love *her*." Eden admitted, slurring the words as she slumped back into the booth.

Erik winced and slid another shot in her direction. "I beg you, don't ever tell her that," he pleaded.

"And why not? What's so wrong with it? She already owns everything that I am, demands it even, but my love is the one thing she doesn't want. Why?" Eden burst, articulating her words with her hands and nearly knocking their drinks over.

Erik made a face, hastily saving their shots from the Angel's flailing arms. "You've already said it, haven't you?"

Eden went quiet, fidgeting under his amusement. "Maybe," she said reluctantly.

Erik made an 'eek' noise and knocked back his own drink. "And I'm guessing it didn't go too well." He stated, not needing Eden's answer to know the truth.

Eden thought back to the night in the club, the way Lilith had looked at her with such conflicted, panicked eyes. "It could've gone worse, but no, it wasn't great." She admitted.

The sex after had been phenomenal though. Eden tipped back her head at the memory; the way Lilith's touch blazed across her skin, the way her lips had parted as she sunk down onto her lover, taking all that the demon was willing to give.

"Enough of that, dove. I can practically feel how wet you are from over here." Erik said, clicking his fingers in front of Eden's face to bring her back to the present.

"Puh-lease, if you had ovaries, they would've exploded all over mister tall, dark, and well-endowed over there," Eden quipped back, pointing over at the nearly nude dancer.

Erik shot her a sultry look and gave a half wave to said dancer. "Yes well, I am my mother's son," he admitted reluctantly, chinking his glass against hers with a devilish grin.

***

"Fuck, yes," Eden moaned around a mouthful of pizza. Erik made a sound of disgust, picking the pineapple off his own slice as he watched her drunken antics with a grin. They were back in the apartment, with Eden leaning heavily on his side and her legs sprawled out over the sofa.

"I thought that demons don't eat," she said curiously, nudging at the incubus with her elbow.

Erik shrugged and licked tomato sauce from his finger, swirling his tongue around the digit and releasing it with a loud pop. "Most can and do. Lilith is just a little particular about anything that might bring her closer to her humanity."

"You love her," Eden stated simply, turning to look up at him with blurry eyes.

Erik shook his head sadly. "I worship her," he corrected. "Just as thousands of others do. There is no loving a monster, Eden. No matter how sweetly she disguises her intentions. In the end, we're all just toys to be discarded."

Eden wanted to argue. Not about being a toy; that part was one hundred percent the truth. Rather, she wanted to refute Erik's claim that she would eventually be thrown aside, replaced or ignored. But then she realised that Erik wasn't referring to her, he was talking about himself.

Eden opened her mouth to reassure him, to tell him that she would not allow it, but a growl from Maxx cut off the words. The undead cat jumped onto the back of the sofa, arching his back and spitting at the air.

"Maxx?" she asked in alarm, searching the apartment when he continued to growl and swipe at the air. "There's no one here, buddy." She tried to comfort him, only for the skeletal creature to screech and pace, circling around the duo protectively.

Erik pulled himself to his feet, a low, rumbling snarl on his parted red lips.

"Erik?" Eden whispered, frightened and confused by the sudden response. Not to mention, way, *way* too drunk to deal with someone trying to kill her right now.

"Is it a demon?" She stuttered, trying to focus her spinning mind and turning stomach.

Erik yanked her up by the front of her shirt, pulling her behind him as his eyes scanned the room. "I don't know. But I'm not stupid enough to ignore the warning," he said, gesturing to the undead cat's agitated motions.

A heavy boom shook the building, threatening to send the pair toppling to the ground. Eden cried out, looking up at the ceiling as her breaths turned hurried and panicked. "The roof," she whispered.

Maxx's body shook and stretched, elongating as his bones grew sharp and deadly as he crouched before her until he was almost as large as a tiger. He opened his mouth, revealing fangs dripping with Hellfire.

"There there, child. You're safe now," A soft voice whispered, the deep timbre soothing and kind as it brushed against her ear. There was something familiar about the voice, something calming and gentle that called for her to lean into its security.

It felt so completely wrong in comparison to the wicked edge of Lilith's sweet cruelty.

"Shit," Erik cursed, his entire form shaking as his illusion shattered, revealing two small leathery wings and tiny, almost non-existent horns. If Eden wasn't so terrified, she would've giggled and cooed at the adorable additions.

Erik dragged her towards the front door, only to stumble back as it opened without so much as a touch. Stood there, bathed in heavenly light, wearing a pure white toga, was a man, and on his back, were two great feathery wings that were overwhelming in their brilliance and divinity. He looked to the demon first, curling his lips in distaste as he raised a fist.

"Erik!" Eden cried, watching as the incubus flew across the room, tipping back the couch as he landed with a heavy grunt.

Maxx charged at the creature with a challenging roar, clamping his fire-tipped fangs around his leg. He wasn't powerful enough to battle an Angel, even with his new additions, but regardless, he would protect his mistress' home, mate, and cub. With his life, if necessary.

The male yelled out in pain, striking Maxx with his wings and shattering every single bone that made up his body.

"Maxx!" Eden screamed, reaching out to the skeletal monstrosity that was her friend.

Another Angel appeared at the entrance to the roof, a woman this time, with a severe face and impatient eyes that tracked Eden's every movement as she ran to Erik's side.

The incubus groaned and pulled his shoulder back into place with a loud pop that made both of them wince. "The coin," he snapped, summoning fire to his hands and spinning it into a tight funnel, shooting it towards the approaching Angels. They didn't even flinch; mortal fire held no effect on them.

Eden frantically fumbled through her pockets and, after a painfully long moment, finally pulled it free. "We-we're under attack; help us!" She pleaded, pulling the coin up to her mouth. "Lucifer!"

The coin's dark aura grew still and speculative for a moment, before fading away, leaving nothing more than a useless lump of metal in her hand.

"You fucking bastard!" Eden screeched, throwing the coin at the approaching Angels. Her wings burst from her back, curling and whipping around her body in response to her fear, flapping frantically and lifting her off the floor.

The female Angel stepped forward; her hands held out soothingly as she spoke. "Come now, little one, it is time to go home," she said, as if she believed Eden to be little more than a child throwing a tantrum at the park.

Erik hissed and bared his fangs, settling his smaller form in front of the frightened Angel protectively. "Over my dead fucking body," he barked. He rather liked the curvy wallflower. There was a spark of stubborn fire under that meek angelic exterior, just waiting to arise.

"Your life has been bargained for, demon spawn, but only if you step aside. Do so, and you might even live to one day get your big boy wings," the woman taunted, her voice startlingly cold in comparison to how she'd spoken to Eden.

Erik wrestled with his sense of self-preservation, but ultimately, loyalty to his mistress and sire won out. He growled low, curling his fingers into deadly claws as he held her eyes.

The angelic pair looked at each other, and the woman sighed and shook her head in disappointment. Her movements were barely more than a blur to the duo. She propelled herself forward, taking Erik's head in her grip and jerking it sideways, breaking his neck like a twig.

A great tremor overtook Eden's body, and she stared in mute horror as Erik's glowing eyes, so very painfully similar to Lilith's, dimmed and faded to a muted grey. Silent tears streaked down her face as she looked between the broken body of her new friend and the shattered remains of Maxx. "You have no *idea* what you have done," she trembled, glaring up at the Angel with a furious gaze. "She will come for me, and she will rip your head from your body."

The woman smiled and gently brushed her hair aside. Eden jerked away from the touch, forcing her frozen body into movement. She beat her fists against the Angel's chest, struck her with her wings, and tried to bite into the arm pulling her forward.

"Hush now, child. She can't hurt you anymore," the woman reassured, but all Eden felt was fury and terror.

Lie.

***

Lucifer stepped out of the shadows and into Lilith's apartment. They frowned, crouching down to pluck their coin from the ground. They lingered briefly, eyeing the body of the blonde-haired boy that Lilith was so fond of, and a sliver of regret churned in their gut.

Lucy brushed the feeling aside to gently place their coin on Lilith's pillow. The succubus would rage for a while, but in time, she would understand. It was for the best.

Chapter 11

"Lucifer, I summon thee," Lilith seethed for the thousandth time, pacing up and down the length of her destroyed apartment.

Erik's body lay in her bed, carefully cocooned in blankets, his broken neck slowly knitting back together under her magic. Healing wasn't exactly her forte, obviously. But soul magic transcended the laws of both light and dark magic. The return of the soul itself was what healed him, as it could not linger in a host without life.

It wasn't difficult to pull him back. For a demon, the boy was irritatingly human hearted.

Once again, Lucy did not appear; did not respond to her summons, and the coin in her hand sat stubbornly silent. For the first time in their long friendship, the Devil had abandoned her.

"*I'm sorry*." The words taunted her, pushing her to the edge again and again under her incomprehension of the apology.

But now she understood.

No matter what she said or did, Lucifer would not appear, not even to offer an apology or explanation.

Lilith roared her rage, the force of it enough to shatter every window, mirror, and surviving piece of crockery in her apartment. Eden was unharmed; she could sense that much. She could feel the soft tugging on her soul that grated against her demonic nature. But it was clouded, shrouded by light magic, and no matter how hard she tried, she could not follow the slight pull.

Her initial instinct had been to charge back into Hell, wring her master's neck, and demand they tell her what they'd done with the Angel. But every time Lilith tried to open a portal to the underworld, she was met an impenetrable wall, further increasing her fury. She could feel the realm's regret, Hell's silent apology, even as it obeyed its master.

Lilith stooped to pick up a small, pearly white feather from the floor, only to screech at the blinding pain and burn that spread over her hand. She stared at the weeping wound in disbelief. This wasn't one of Eden's feathers, she realised with a sinking heart.

Lilith picked it up again, clenching her fist around the feather even as her flesh blackened and smoked from the contact. She growled. If Lucy wanted to play at giving her the silent treatment, then she would make herself impossible to ignore.

***

Eden sat still and silent at the elaborately decorated vanity. The female Angel, Gabriel, hovered close, ever present and dotingly gentle, as she ran her fingers through Eden's wavy brown hair, adjusted her wings, or righted her dress.

On paper, everything should be perfect. But Eden couldn't swallow the bile that rose in her throat. Something was missing.

Someone was missing.

Eden didn't know what or who; all she knew was that there was a pain in her heart, an emptiness and frustration in her body that begged to be filled and taken.

"I don't belong here," she murmured, looking up to the older Angel beseechingly for an explanation.

"This is your home," Gabriel said firmly, leaving no room for any further argument. "This is where you belong."

Lie.

***

The demon under Lilith's boot gave a gargled choke and fell still, his eyes rolling into the back of his head as he left his human host. Erik watched from the sidelines, a slight grimace on his face at the sight of Lilith's heel sticking through the man's neck.

"How many are we on tonight?" She asked lowly, wiping her bloody boot on the human's shirt.

"Twenty-three," Erik said shortly, too frightened to risk one of his usual smart remarks. The succubus was becoming increasingly unpredictable in Eden's absence, and not to mention, violent.

Lilith snarled at his tone, snapping her teeth at the little blonde incubus for his insolence. Eden's disappearance sat like an ever-present weight on her heart and sanity, pushing and pulling on her restraint. Cruelty, madness, and rage was all she knew, and even half starved,

Lilith was intent on making sure that the entirety of the supernatural world knew it too.

The parade Eden wanted to go to was today, and Lilith was tempted to go and butcher a protester or two just out of spite. She could already see Eden's exasperated look in her mind's eye; could hear the high pitch of the Angel's voice as she scolded her murderous actions.

Lilith would've smiled and teased; would've pulled her Angel close with a kiss that would've left her panting, all thoughts of rebuke gone from her tongue.

But instead, she was alone, spiralling into a grief she didn't even realise she could feel, drowning in a rage that threatened to burn the world.

"It's not enough," Lilith snapped, only feeling the slightest trace of guilt as Erik hunched further into himself in fear.

Lucy wouldn't so much as acknowledge her, though she knew she still held their protection based on the way the Hell-born demons on earth responded to her. Namely, screaming in terror and running for the hills.

Not that it got them very far.

A small measure of guilt nagged at the back of her mind. While she enjoyed battle and bloodshed, it was rare that her murderous actions were unprompted.

Lilith pushed the guilt aside, ruling in favour of the rage that continued to eat at her conscience. After a further sixteen kills, none of whom were deserving of her retribution, she reluctantly returned to her apartment with Erik in tow. The incubus lingered on the edges of her space, too wary of attracting her attention to venture further inside.

He missed Eden. The plump Angel may not think so, but she softened Lilith's sharp edges, allowing a small trace of humanity to build in her soul.

Waving the boy away, Lilith poured a small amount of rum into a glass. She set the decanter down, sighed, and picked it back up, drinking straight from the bottle.

Lilith twirled Lucy's coin over her fingers absently as she thought. Thick black circles lingered beneath her eyes, and her cheeks, while usually sharp, sat hollowed and grey on her face. Her body almost shook with hunger, but Lilith would not feed, not when that meant betraying her sweet Angel lover.

"All these years, I gave you so much. I gave you all of me – everything you ever asked for – and you couldn't just allow me this *one fucking thing*," she whispered aimlessly, brushing her lips over Lucy's coin.

But as always, her words were met with silence. "I will *never* forgive you for this."

***

Eden hummed a pretty tune under her breath as she watched the harpist masterfully pluck her fingers over the strings. It was awful, truly. The sound was akin to nails on a chalkboard to her ears, despite its melodic beauty.

Gabriel sat close by, her hawk-like eyes ever trained on Eden's actions, looking for any sign of a lingering memory.

When a lesser Angel, known as a Cupid, floated passed with a handful of cut lilies, Eden sat upright, making to follow her.

"Edera," Gabriel called, a command that went ignored as Eden reached out to snatch a flower from the Cupid's hand.

"Where are my lilies?" She mumbled, her mind spiralling into a mess of confusion and anger at the sight of the innocuous flower.

Gabriel tried to pull her away, only to yelp as Eden's wings burst from her back, striking her in the face and sending her tumbling to the ground. The surrounding Angels gasped and paused, preparing to intervene, only to be waved away by Gabriel. They didn't dare disobey the revered Archangel, so they lingered at the sides, their wings ruffling curiously as they watched the struggle.

"Where are my lilies?" Eden repeated frantically, tearing the flower in her grip into tiny pieces. Gabriel all but dragged her from the great cathedral-like chamber, bringing Eden into her arms as the young Angel's knees buckled under the weight of her grief.

Eden's words soon transformed as her mind began to shatter under the spell containing her memories.

From, "where are my lilies?" To, "where's my Lilly?" She shrieked, struggling against the Archangel holding her close.

Gabriel grit her teeth in frustration. This was the fourth time Eden had broken through the spell of erasure. Lilith's wicked hold over the young Angel was stronger than she'd thought. But rather than somehow believing it was love and devotion breaking through the spell, Gabriel felt nothing but pity and concern for Eden as she imagined the tortures the girl must've endured at the demon's hand to leave such an imprint.

"You're safe; you're safe now, youngling," she tried to comfort, wilfully ignoring Eden's every protest.

Gabriel summoned Charmaine to once again renew the spell of erasure, the other Angel's face mirroring her concern and frustration at the situation.

"We will damage her mind if this continues, Gabriel," Charmaine warned, even as she took Eden's head into her palms, weaving her gift over the young Angel's mind.

Charmaine sighed and looked down at the girl sadly. What she was doing was a violation; a complete and total invasion of privacy and autonomy, but she would not deny Gabriel's request.

"It is for the best, my love," Gabriel said firmly. "Look at what the weight of her memories does to her; she is better off forgetting."

"Lilly!" Eden cried, ugly tears and snot covering her face as she sought to hold onto the memories that were once again being locked away. The light of her feathers began to dim. They started to fall, shedding from her wings in small clumps in response to her ignored turmoil.

The spell took hold, and Eden's eyes went blank and placid once more. She smiled up at her captor, hesitantly placing her hand in Charmaine's as the Archangel gently pulled her to her feet.

"Did I fall?" she asked sweetly, her face clouded in confused.

"Don't worry, little one," Gabriel cooed, gently stroking her fingers through Eden's hair as she turned to Charmine with a grateful smile. "We caught you just in time."

Lilith watched with a grim face as The Devil's Dealings burnt to the ground in a maelstrom of Hellfire, the screams from those within haunting even her. There were innocents in there, women she'd fucked and enjoyed numerous times, demons that she could loosely consider friendly acquaintances.

But none of them mattered.

"Am I to be next then?" Erik asked quietly. There wasn't a single demon left in the territory, Lilith had decimated the lot. And yet, their King still did not show.

Lilith half turned to the incubus, trying to call upon what little feeling she had left to reassure him. A few of her other creations had fallen to her anger, but no. Not this one. Never this one.

Without speaking, Lilith turned away again, her once beautiful face alight with the furious blue glow of Hellfire and grief.

Eden rubbed the red petal between her fingers curiously. Heaven's infinite courtyard was insufferably white. White paths, white pillars, white benches, and white flowers.

All bar one.

Gabriel called to her, beckoning Eden back to her side, '*where she belonged.*'

A lie. Eden could feel it in her bones. But she did not know how, and she did not know why. So she followed along, quiet and docile under Gabriel's commanding gaze.

Eden picked the vibrant red rose, stuffing it beneath the top of her dress, right between her breasts. She was captivated by the colour, the rich hue that pulled a wicked smile and sharp fangs to mind, turning her legs to jelly and warming her in the strangest, most confusing of ways.

"Edera, you must return to your lessons," Gabriel scolded, pulling her back onto the bench and fussing over the creases in her dress.

Eden stifled an eye roll. Heaven forbid her dress not be perfect while she studied. Eden flinched and looked around warily, certain that someone might've heard her inner blasphemy. But no one said anything, so Eden tested it again.

'God damn it,' she thought, wincing slightly as she waited to be struck down for her insolence. Gabriel didn't seem to notice, nor did the numerous Angels surrounding them, but Eden felt the slightest trickle of amusement brush against her mind.

"*You don't belong here, little one,*" It whispered, the voice curling through her consciousness before fading away completely.

***

Upon Lilith's bedside table, the decapitated head of Hell's representative to the Worldwide Supernatural Council sat with her mouth agape and frozen in pain, even in death.

A rash action, one that would ultimately have consequences when the pompous fools realised what she'd done. But it didn't matter. All that mattered was the return of her Angel to her side, consequences be damned.

A rare smile split Lilith's chapped lips as the shadows of the room grew violent and twisted, signifying the return of her exalted 'master.'

"Many thanks," she said, tipping her glass to the severed head sarcastically.

"You go too far," Lucifer growled, storming out of the mass of swirling darkness.

Lilith took another swig of her drink, her tongue darting out to catch the stray droplet that dribbled from her lips. She rose slowly, not looking at the furious face of her master as she retrieved the stray feather from between her breasts. The skin there was scarred and pink, probably permanently, from the light magic that screamed as it came into contact with her demonic nature.

"This tantrum has gone on long enough. You will cease this senseless rampage, Lilith; I demand it." Lucy ordered, their voice rising in anger as Lilith merely continued to finger the feather in her grasp, not even deigning to look at them. "Are you even listening to me?" They snapped. "Hell is in outrage at your actions."

"I AM IN OUTRAGE!" Lilith exploded, her calm exterior breaking into sudden chaos. *"Me!"* She beat her fist against her chest to emphasise the point.

Lucifer reeled back from the magic thrumming in the room as Lilith's breasts heaved in fury. While they were undeniably more powerful than the succubus, they were not foolish enough to believe that a physical confrontation with her would end well. They may win, but in the end, the cost would be severe.

"Lilith," they went to scold irritably, only for the succubus to screech and throw her glass, shattering it against their form.

"Do not presume to speak my name, you fucking traitor. What have you done?" Lilith demanded, holding up the feather and thrusting it into their face.

"She is where she belongs," they said stubbornly, meeting Lilith's fury with a calmness that only inflamed her ire.

"She belongs with me. She is mine! She is my breath and heart. She is whatever remains of my twisted, shrivelled soul, and **you took her**." Lilith raged, speaking over her master's attempts to calm her.

"Heaven took her," Lucifer argued on a technicality. Lilith snatched up everything in reach, throwing the objects at the bastard who called themself her 'friend.'

"They may have been the ones to take her, but as always, you, the grand puppet master, held the FUCKING STRINGS. You call yourself my friend, protector, and master, and yet all you do is push and pull me this way and that in an effort to control my actions. You're no better than he is," Lilith said bitterly, taking her head into her hands and raking her claws down her own face when they only shook their head condescendingly.

"I have played into your petty, dramatic little games for countless millennia because I thought you were my friend. Because I... because I..." Lilith choked on her words and her fury broke, her face dropping as a gasping sob tumbled from her lips. "Because *I love you*," she whispered brokenly, uttering words she'd never been able to before. "With whatever is left of me that can love. And I trusted that you loved me too."

"I do; you are my finest creation," Lucy said, trying to bring Lilith into their arms.

The succubus screamed again, a sound of frustration and hurt, and she cut the Devil off once more. "I was never your fucking creation. I am not Hell's, not Heaven's, not Earth's. I am my own creation. And I chose to give myself to Eden. **Me**! I chose. And you took that from me."

"She will be your undoing!" They finally yelled back, "her mere presence brings danger to your door."

"You *will* help me secure her return," Lilith growled threateningly, striking her finger into Lucy's half formed body.

"Or what? What will you do?" They challenged. Lucy stared the succubus down, daring her to speak the words that were clear on the tip of her tongue. A challenge she didn't back away from.

"Or I will rain fire and death upon every demon that walks this earth. If you think that Hell is in outrage now, just imagine the rebellion I will spark, the armies I will be able to raise – against you, for the breaking of a pact made in blood. And you know what? You can't fucking stop me." Lilith whispered, stepping into their space with a dark gleam in her dimmed, starving eyes.

"You would threaten your master? I give you your power, your security!" Lucifer retorted, coming dangerously close to speaking words that could not be taken back. But unlike Lilith, they couldn't bear to speak them aloud.

Lilith threw back her head and laughed while brushing her tears aside. "I am primordial. My power is my own; that was your decree to me at the beginning of time in exchange for my hand. That was our bargain struck, and even the Devil themself cannot break their word without consequences," she spat, locking their eyes in a battle that continued in silence.

"You would break us, break our friendship for some pathetic, mewling little girl whose mere existence amounts to seconds in comparison?" They asked quietly, their face stricken with pain.

"I have given you everything I have. My devotion, my loyalty, my care. I gave you my eternity." Lilith paused for breath, heaving deeply as she tried to settle her frantically whirring mind. "What more do you want? I asked only for her, and in exchange, you have betrayed me." She stumbled over the words, choking back the furious sob that fought to fall free.

"Eden *hates* you, truly, loathes you. But she is not the one forcing my hand, not the one breaking my heart by asking me to choose. So yes, I choose her," she said, settling their argument definitively, even though it cleaved her blackened heart in half.

Lucy's shadowed form wavered and broke into wisps of smoke before reforming once more. They were smaller now, more fragile looking.

"If you go to her, I cannot protect you. You will barely be more than mortal in the divine realm," they whispered mournfully, reaching out to brush their touch between Lilith's breasts, healing the mottled scar that lingered there from the feather still gripped between her fingers.

"That is my choice to make. Will you take that from me too?" She asked, daring them to say no. They remained quiet for a moment, testing the validity of her resolve, and then they sighed.

***

Lucifer stormed back through the gates of hell, disappearing and reappearing in a puff of smoke before their throne. They paced, their movements choppy and uncoordinated before the court. "Prepare my legions," they commanded quietly.

Alister blinked up at them, confusion evident on his blue tinged face. "How many, My liege?" He asked, lowering his eyes from the throne and his master.

"All of them!" Lucifer roared, the force of it shaking the entire realm. If Lilith was intent on this course of action, something that wouldn't be necessary without their underhanded deal with Gabriel, then Lucy would make sure that the armies of Hell were prepared for the inevitable fallout.

Chapter 12

Eden watched herself in the mirror. Lesser Angels fussed over her hair and dress, getting her ready for the grand celebration due to start any second.

Apparently her 'return' was something of a big deal. Return from where, Eden didn't know. Her hair fell long and curled, held back by a small golden circlet with a round, twinkling white jewel that dropped over her forehead.

The dress was pretty enough, if a little bland and unbearably white. Everyone in Heaven seemed to wear some variation of the same toga or stola, something that made Eden want to giggle and roll her eyes.

She didn't know why; it just seemed so… so very *cliché.*

When the chattering Cupids finally left the room to fetch her escort, Eden pulled the creased red rose from under her pillow. She returned to the mirror and held it up to her neck. There was something missing, something that should be sat red and angry upon her skin, marking her for everyone to see.

But all Eden had was the single rose, the vibrant hue sending a twisting ache between her legs at the echo of a memory lingering just out of reach. She picked a petal and brought it up to her mouth, pressing it between her lips and holding it there. She pulled it free and smiled at the faint colour staining her lips. That's better.

There was a knock at the door, and Eden hastily stuffed the rose back between her breasts lest she be caught with the offending colour. Gabriel entered without waiting for a response, looking as regal and as severe as always, something that gentled somewhat as she looked upon Eden with approval.

"Do you like it?" Eden asked shyly, spinning the draping fabric around her legs.

Gabriel tutted and frowned, wiping at the red stain on the young Angel's lips. "Vanity calls Pride," she scolded. "We are above such things, Edera."

Lie.

That's not my name, Eden wanted to say. She wanted to scream and shout it for all of Heaven to hear. But instead, she followed the woman from the room, obediently trailing behind her as they made their way through Heaven's grand court.

Tapestries woven in gold and magic hung from the walls; elegant statues of heroes and Angels stood stationed throughout, their magnificence amplified by the unrelenting glow of Heaven's realm.

Eden forced a fresh smile onto her face as those around her spoke, not to her, but at her. They drawled on about things she didn't understand or care about. They spoke of a place called Earth, about demons and war, and then they laughed, as if it was all one great big joke. It sat heavy and bitter in her stomach, the way they brushed the subject aside as if it no longer mattered.

Eden waited for Gabriel's vigilant attention to shift before retreating to the fringes of the party. Lesser Angels kept their wings tucked close or completely concealed, she observed with a faint frown. Whereas the High Angels and Archangels like Gabriel, kept theirs unfurled and raised. The word manspreading came to mind, and Eden choked back her laughter.

"You don't belong here," a heavy voice whispered into her ear.

Eden gasped and tried to turn, but there was no one there. Power lingered in the words, filled by an omniscient force that curled around her mind.

"I know," she whispered in return, staring down at the golden chalice in her hand. "Where do I belong?" she asked quietly, desperately seeking some sort of answer for the turmoil in her mind. The voice did not respond. It faded away like a dying sun on winters night, as if it had never even existed at all, leaving Eden to her silent contemplation.

"Edera," Gabriel called, holding out her hand for Eden to rejoin the party. She swallowed her reluctance, hesitantly allowing the Angel to tug her back into the crowd with a fake smile curling on her lips.

"Why don't you go and dance?" Gabriel commanded, disguising it as a question.

'Why don't you kiss my ass?' Eden wanted to say. But instead, she nodded and flapped her wings, clumsily flying to the floating dance floor above. Those around her cooed and laughed softly at her ungainly flight, fondly remembering their own struggles as their confidence in the air grew.

She was barely an infant in their eyes; new to life and struggling to find herself as she learned what it meant to exist in their world. The mortal body would have to go, they all agreed, eager to see the budding Archangel unfurl her wings and unleash her full potential.

Eden joined the dance on unsteady feet, raising her arms above her head as she followed the ridiculously formal steps.

A flash of something caught her eye, and Eden skipped a step to turn, earning irritated glances from those around her as she broke formation. Eden didn't care; all of her focus was narrowed in on a single form.

A woman, with long, lustrous black hair and a feathered white mask, circled the edges of the dance floor with a sharp, predatory smile. The sight stalled the breath in her lungs, frantically calling for her heart to pound and race at the woman's mere presence.

Eden fumbled to rejoin the dance, gasping in pain as she spun and lost sight of the figure for a brief moment. It was like a knife to the heart, twisting and pulling at her chest until she returned her gaze to the dark-haired beauty once more.

She met Eden's eyes, and the Angel whimpered at the startling wrongness of the pale blue irises. Gesturing for her to follow with a single curled finger, the woman backed away, her gaze never once leaving Eden's as she slowly floated from the room.

As if in a trance, Eden cut across the dance floor to follow. There was a pull in her gut, in her mind, and between her legs that demanded she go to the raven-haired beauty immediately. Rounding the corner, Eden almost screamed as a hand wrapped around her throat to pin her to the cold marble wall.

"Naughty, naughty girl, this doesn't look like hands and knees to me, pet." The woman purred, pressing their bodies together.

Confusion wrestled with something hot and wanting in her body. "Is that my name?" Eden asked with relief at finally feeling something *right.*

Pet. Pet. Pet. Her mind churned the word on repeat. *Yes.*

The woman pulled back, pressing her chillingly cold palm to Eden's plump cheek. "Oh, pretty girl, what have they done to you?" She asked, her voice stricken as she clenched her hand tighter around the Angel's neck.

"I think I know you," Eden slurred, her words and mind becoming thick with confusion as it battled against the magic stretching over it. "I think I love you." Her body seemed to have a mind of its own; it arched into the violent touch, seeking to become impossibly closer to the woman holding her against the wall.

"Oh, my treasure," The woman breathed, staring down at Eden with a tenderness that didn't match the possessive hand wrapped around her throat. "You know what you want, pet. Trust me and take it."

Eden got the feeling that this creature was the last person in existence she should trust. But, God, it feel so very right. She wound her arms around the woman's neck, gently pressing a kiss to those tauntingly red lips. They both moaned at the contact, both starving and empty in completely different ways, and the brief touch only inflamed their hunger.

Eden deepened the kiss, the touch of their tongues like fireworks over her skin, superheating her body and bringing colour back to the world. "I think – I think –" Eden gasped between kisses.

"Don't think, just feel me," the stranger growled, pulling Eden's hands to her body.

The Angel welcomed the mouth dominating her own with a greedy whine. Pressure built, mounting higher and higher, pressing on Eden's mind until finally, the dam broke, unleashing a torrent of scenes behind her eyes of another life, one in which she belonged solely to the creature before her.

"Lilly," Eden panted, pulling back to look up at the woman in awe. "You came for me."

Lilith gave a breathless smile and firmly pressed her thumb to Eden's mouth, smearing the stained red lipstick there in a bid to press her claim back over the Angel.

"White is not your colour," Eden giggled suddenly, and Lilith laughed into her hair, her own joy plain to see as she clung to the delicious curves of her pet's body. "Lilly, your eyes." Eden's words were filled with such pained sorrow as she traced the shadows beneath the succubus' eyes, gently brushing her fingertips over the purple hue.

"Shh shh," Lilith hushed, bringing Eden back into another searing kiss.

Lilith had thought that sneaking into Heaven would be far more difficult, but the pompous chickens were either stupid or ridiculously self-assured. As it turned out, Lucy, the very naughty Devil, had squirrelled away just enough of their divinity to open a one-time portal to Heaven.

How they would return to earth, Lilith had no clue, but that seemed like a problem to deal with later. Right now, she was far too consumed by the sweet Angel clutching at the front of her sickeningly white dress.

"Fuck, here?" Eden groaned when Lilith dropped to her knees to hike up her dress. The succubus shot her a wicked grin, running her tongue over her fangs as she lifted Eden's leg to rest on her shoulder.

"Lilith, we've got to go-*oh*!" Eden gasped, clamping her hand over her mouth to muffle the noise.

Lilith let loose a rumbling growl as she breathed in the sweet scent of Eden's arousal. She brushed her nose over the soft patch of hair between the Angel's legs, fighting every instinct that screamed for her to sink her fangs into the soft flesh.

Not yet, she cautioned herself. Lucifer's scraps of divinity could only conceal so much. The second she fed and grew stronger; the others would sense her presence.

"I have been so cold without you, so empty," Lilith murmured, swiping her tongue through the pink folds under her mouth, lapping up the evidence of the Angel's desire.

Eden gasped and fisted a hand in her hair. "Don't tease me, not now!" She whined, her eyes darting to the end of the hallway and the celebration beyond. All it would take was one stray, curious Angel, and they would be exposed.

Lilith chuckled and ignored the plea, moving her mouth to nip at Eden's thighs, leaving small red bruises on the skin.

Eden smacked her head back on the marbled wall as Lilith swirled her tongue around the outside of her clit, building the tension in her body to near unrivalled heights.

Lilith smirked and took more of Eden's weight as she gently lifted the hood of her clit to flatten her tongue to the aching bud of nerves. She started off light, gradually increasing the pressure and speed as Eden shook and clenched around her head, holding her in place.

"*Oh!* Fuck yes," Eden trembled, her body curling and tensing as waves of pleasure began to ebb and flow through her body, a sensation she didn't realise she was in withdrawal from until she finally tipped over the edge of release.

Lilith grunted at the sudden weight on her shoulders as Eden slumped against the wall. She pressed one last lingering kiss to Eden's clit and pulled her head free from under the Angel's dress.

Eden slid down the wall, pulling Lilith into her arms and pressing the succubus to her breast as their legs entwined. "I cannot bear your pain," she whispered, begging for the succubus to feast upon her soul.

Unable to resist the gentle plea, Lilith pulled Eden's dress down to sink her fangs into the soft flesh of her breast, and she moaned as the Angel's soul leeched into her mouth.

Power thrummed in her blood, but it held little weight in Heaven. Even now, Lilith could feel the oppressive light magic prickling over her entire body, rendering her weak and barely more than mortal.

Eden's lips parted at the pleasurably painful sensation. She stroked Lilith's hair, coaxing the woman to take her fill. If the succubus decided that this was the time she devoured her entirely, then Eden would meet her fate with open arms.

Some might call her delusional or pathetic, a simpering wallflower who obeyed and stood useless as she was tugged this way and that.

But the truth was, Eden could stop Lilith at any point. She just didn't want to. And as poor of a decision as it might seem, it was *hers* to make.

Eden could feel the tugging on her soul, its steady decline as she was devoured whole, and she could feel the exact moment when it would become too late to stop. If she was to die one day, then this was the only way she would go. In the arms of the woman she loved.

Just as she hit the threshold, Lilith pulled back, swiping her tongue over Eden's breast to clean the small trickle of blood leaking from the wound.

They smiled at each other, basking in the lingering warmth and electricity sparking between them. A soft, contented purr vibrated in Lilith's chest, and the demon for once welcomed the noise, for it meant that this was real, and her pet was finally back in her arms.

"I treasure you," Eden teased sweetly, peppering the succubus's face with chaste kisses.

Lilith laughed lowly, her face lighter and burden free once more as she returned to her full beauty. "I love you," she said quietly in return, the words holding more weight than the Earth itself, and Eden was surprised to see a trace of vulnerability in those piercing blue eyes.

"Good, because you're stuck with me," Eden declared, wiping her own cheeks when she realised she was crying.

"Oh dear, however will I cope?" Lilith drawled sarcastically, offering her hand to the Angel and pulling the woman to her feet.

"Don't get me wrong, I'm overjoyed to see you, but how are you even here?" Eden asked as Lilith tugged her further down the hallway.

The succubus poked her head around the corner, continuing on with a wary eye as the hair on the back of her neck stood on end. "Maybe we should save the explanations for another time, pet. They'll be able to sense me now that I've fed," Lilith said, and Eden bit her tongue to hold the retort lingering on the end.

Considering Lilith was the one who had insisted on fucking her against the wall, it was more than a little humorous to Eden that she couldn't spare a single second to explain what the hell was going on.

All seemed quiet at first, but then, like some over-dramatic jailbreak scene in a crappy movie, Heaven erupted in activity. Guardians, the warrior Angels of old, rushed them from both sides, smacking their spears against their shields in an attempt to intimidate the demon.

Lilith snarled and flashed her fangs. She tried to summon Hellfire to her hands, but the force couldn't spark to life in the divine realm. Her wings had faded to ash the second she'd crossed the portal, so she lashed out with her claws, raking them over the Guardian's ridiculously shiny armour.

Honestly, if she was forced into wearing something that uncomfortable for all eternity, she'd probably be a little grouchy too.

"Lilith!" Eden startled, reaching for the demon as Gabriel appeared, wrapping her arms around Eden's thick waist and pulling the young Angel away.

Lilith was like a feral animal, all savagery and instinct to kill as she struck at the Angels daring to touch what belonged to her.

"Let me go, let me go! Lilith!" Eden shrieked.

They came so close, their fingers barely millimetres from touching before the butt of a spear came down hard on Lilith's face, knocking her head to the side and breaking her nose with a blow that sent a spray of black blood onto the pristine white floor.

"Lilith!" Eden cried, watching her love fall at the feet of the Guardians who continued striking her.

Chapter 13

Lilith moaned weakly as she awoke to an endless array of voices and cheers. She opened her eyes, only to blink rapidly and wince at the overwhelming brightness surrounding her.

"The guest of honour finally graces us by awakening," a long-dreaded voice snarked.

Lilith closed her eyes and blew a long puff of air from her slowly healing nose. She tried to move, but she was bound tight, chained to the floor before the denizens of Heaven.

Lilith's eyes sought out Eden's on instinct, and she burned at the sight of her beautiful wings tied to her back, unable to spread or fly. Tears streaked down the Angel's face as she looked up at the demon onstage, but she could not move. Where Lilith's bonds were blessed, Eden's own were cursed.

'Lilly,' she mimed, her voice horse and sore from screaming.

Lilith smiled at her softly, not allowing her own helplessness and fear to show on her face.

No matter the outcome of this, Eden would live. They weren't going to kill or clip the wings of an Angel so young. This would all be chalked up to a youthful indiscretion, and while miserable, Eden's life would be infinite in Heaven's crushing hold.

"I see you're still a little touchy, Gabriel. Maybe you should've taken me up on my offer and let me bend you over the remains of Sodom. It might've loosened the stick up your ass… or pushed it deeper, whatever your preference." Lilith's words cut off into a pained screech as the Angel pressed her wing to her face.

Gabriel fisted a hand in Lilith's hair, baring her burnt face for the crowd to see, but the demon swallowed her cries at the sight of Eden's tear-streaked face.

"You never did know when to quit, Lilith," the Angel whispered into her ear, throwing her forward and raising a hand for the crowd to still. "Welcome, Brothers and Sisters. We, God's most devout children, are gathered here today for a most solemn event. Read the charges," Gabriel ordered the lesser Angel lingering by her side.

The Angel cleared his throat. "Lilith, Queen Consort of Hell, The First Woman, The First True Demon, Mistress of Darkness, Mother of–"

"Oh, for God's sake, just get on with it already! I'll die of boredom before you lot finish with those fucking titles," Lilith called, rolling her eyes at the pompous display.

Little fucking hypocrites.

They liked to proclaim themselves above mortal sin, but all Lilith could see was evidence of their Pride, Greed, Gluttony, and Envy. At least she owned her wickedness instead of hiding it behind a veil of purity and light.

The crowd gasped and raged at her blasphemous words, calling for the head of the Demon they were all taught to fear.

Gabriel merely tightened her lips and snatched the scroll back from the stumped lesser Angel. "Your sins are without end. And today, your long-endured amnesty comes to an end. You stand accused of the murder of hundreds of thousands of souls, the imprisonment and enslavement of an Angel, the brutalisation of an Angel, and finally, the rape of an Angel. For these crimes, you will be sentenced to total destruction. How do you plead?" Gabriel asked, her lips curling further in disgust with every word that she spoke.

She would bring Eden justice by delivering Lilith's head to Hell, and the young Angel would finally be free of her tormentor.

No, no, no, no! That wasn't right!

Eden tried to lurch forward, tried to join her love onstage and proclaim her innocence, at least, to the last three charges.

"She's lying; somebody, please believe me, she's lying!" Eden cried, fighting against her bonds.

The crowd shook their heads pityingly at the poor creature, so brainwashed by the darkness she was steeped in that she truly believed the words she was speaking.

Lilith pulled herself back to her knees and grinned at the bloodthirsty crowd. "Guilty," she said proudly, baring her fangs. It didn't matter what she said, they were going to execute her anyway. At least this way, her words would further cloak Eden in innocence.

Lie. Lie. Lie.

"Joseph," Gabriel called, spreading her wings wide for the crowd to see. The Archangel Joseph stepped forward; a blazing sword engulfed in fire in his hand. He placed it into position, lingering just over the demon's neck as he waited for the command to strike.

There would be no coming back from this.

The flaming sword of the creator didn't just kill the body; it annihilated the very essence and soul.

Lilith's glowing blue eyes stayed locked onto Eden's, willing them to be the last thing she saw before she was destroyed. She smiled, forcing her face to show every tender moment, every soft feeling of affection that she'd pushed down or hidden.

"You're going to be okay," Lilith whispered, solely meant for the woman she loved.

Gabriel nodded her head, and Joseph swung the sword down.

"**Liar!**" Eden roared, her voice reverberating around the great chamber, vibrating through the air with a shattering boom that brought everyone to their knees.

Divine light rippled from her chest, searing through the cursed chains wrapped around her wings, and obliterating the blessed bonds tethering Lilith to the stage. Heaven itself shook under the force, and Eden took to the sky, using the momentary distraction to go to Lilith's side.

Lilith sucked in a shaky breath and shook at the sight of the flaming sword sticking out of the ground, barely inches from her head.

"Fuck me, that was close," She laughed, turning to meet Eden's furious gaze with a delirious grin. The Angel lashed out, smacking her across the face with a sharp slap.

"Guilty?" Eden hissed, pulling the demon to her feet as those around them struggled to do the same. "What were you thinking, you egotistical sociopath?"

"I was thinking my sweet little bird needed a push," Lilith cooed, concealing her own fear at the near destruction. There had been a few close calls over the course of her long life, but none had shaken her quite so much.

"I'll be pushed into strangling you one day," Eden snapped, flapping her wings in an attempt to bring them both into the air. It was a lot harder than Lilith made it look. Eden barely made it a foot off the ground before Gabriel tackled them back to the stage.

"Oh, come on!" She yelled, hiking up her dress to kick the Archangel in the face. Gabriel grunted, but once again succeeded in separating the pair as she dragged Eden to safety.

"Enough of this," Lilith snarled. She pulled the flaming sword free from the stage, snaring a lesser Angel from the crowd and holding it to his throat.

Angels fled from the scene as an uncountable number of Guardians flooded the chamber, each of them pointing their spears directly at the demon trespassing in their realm. They reached a stalemate, both parties with their own hostage.

"Kill her. She won't do it. Not even she wants to see the universe burn, not if it means Eden burns too," Gabriel ordered, calling Lilith's bluff.

All Angels were protected by the treaty in their own realm, just the same as all demons were in Hell. It was only on Earth that the rules got a little *dicey.* If Lilith slit the lesser Angel's throat, then chaos would reign across all planes of existence.

Lilith giggled.

Honest to God, giggled.

Eden didn't think she'd ever heard anything more terrifying. The sound was manic and uncontrollable, alluding to the madness sparkling in her iridescent blue eyes.

"You know, it truly baffles me how sure you heavenly hypocrites are in your idiocy," Lilith mocked, bringing the flaming sword flush to the weeping Angel's neck. "It is true; I love Eden," She declared proudly. "And I love the world, in all of its dark, sinful glory. But don't think for a second that I won't do it. If I can't have her, then no one will," she threatened in a sickeningly sweet voice.

"Return my pet and open a *god-damned* portal, or I start the ancient war anew. I will set the world ablaze, dance in the ashes of its destruction, and delight in bringing every creature in this universe as much terror and pain as it brings me to be parted from her."

Truth.

Eden all but swooned. That had to be the most romantic thing she'd ever heard. "Oh Lilly," she whispered, her heart fluttering frantically in her chest as her eyes teared up at the beautiful words.

The surrounding Angels looked at her, completely aghast by her reaction. Eden may have told them, may have proclaimed her love and devotion to the succubus for all to hear. But they'd taken it as nothing more than the brainwashed ramblings of a confused and abused victim. But seeing her now, many thought that she may just be as monstrous as the woman who claimed her.

Gabriel faltered, glancing between Eden and the sword in Lilith's hand. The tension rose, neither side wanting to back down.

"Release him, and I will open a portal," she eventually agreed through gritted teeth. She couldn't risk bringing war; it was the whole reason they'd taken Eden from Earth in the first place. It was just too dangerous for her there.

Lilith tutted and held up a finger, wiggling it chidingly. "See dearest... I just don't trust you. How about this, open a portal and once we're on our merry way, I'll throw the boy back through?" She countered, pointing at Eden, who was still locked in Gabriel's grip.

The Archangel hissed out a breath between her teeth, and a tense silence overtook the gleaming white chamber.

"Tick Tok," Lilith taunted, clucking her tongue to imitate a clock.

"Very well," Gabriel growled, practically throwing Eden away. She stumbled, just barely righting herself as she strained to run to the demon's side.

Lilith hissed at the action and fought the impulse to sweep Eden into her arms. She kept the sword to the simpering boy's neck, grinning up at Gabriel in challenge. "I'm waiting, sweetie," she purred, snapping her fangs close to the lesser Angel's cheek.

Gabriel seethed, spreading her arms and wings wide, summoning a swirling portal made of light magic and golden dust.

Lilith eyed it shrewdly, satisfied to see her still destroyed apartment and Erik's shell-shocked face on the other side. "In you go, pet," she commanded softly, not breaking eye contact with the furious Archangel.

Eden licked her lips and looked at the faces surrounding her. "Put him down, Lilly, please?" She beseeched, stretching her hand out to the demon in offer as she lingered before the portal. "Come home with me."

Eden's mind flashed back to the night Lilith murdered Lisa, and a sinking feeling of de ja vu twisted in her gut. But to her eternal relief, Lilith stepped towards her, her grasp on the lesser Angel loosening enough that he could slip free.

Eden beamed and carefully took the sword from Lilith's hand, intending to drop it to the ground. They went to step through the portal, finally free to return to the earthly plane, when a furious battle cry sounded from behind.

Eden acted on impulse. Time seemed to slow as she spun, lifting the sword to protect the powerless woman at her side.

Heaven froze. In fact, all of creation froze at the sight of an Angel striking down one of her own as Gabriel was impaled on the flaming sword.

The Archangel looked up at Eden, betrayal and confusion evident on her severe face, as if she couldn't fully comprehend what was happening.

Eden herself stood gasping and stunned, unable to believe what she'd just done.

"Fuck," Lilith cursed, wrestling the sword from Eden's startled hands to tackle her back through the shrinking portal. It closed behind them with a sharp 'pop,' its power dying along with the Angel who summoned it, cutting off the enraged screams of the beings on the other side.

Eden's chest heaved as she stared down at her hands. There was no blood; she felt like there should be. She'd stabbed someone. "Lilly," she stuttered, her entire body erupting with chills at the knowledge of what she'd just done.

Lilith herself sat frozen and struck with disbelief at the mental image of her sweet, kind-hearted pet impaling one of the most powerful Archangels in existence. A rush of desire coiled between her legs, but when Eden whimpered and curled into herself, she pushed it down. Now probably wasn't the best time to give in to battle-lust.

"First one is always the hardest, pet," Lilith murmured, sweeping the shaking Angel into her arms. "You didn't mean to," she tried to console a little lamely, not knowing what else to say.

Eden just shook her head.

"I meant to," she admitted through shaking sobs, looping her arms around Lilith's neck as the woman carried her to bed.

Blankets wound around her, nearly smothering her in their warmth, and Eden kicked them aside in favour of the soothing cold of Lilith's arms. "I broke the treaty. I've killed us all," she fretted, her wide, watery eyes staring up at the succubus in fear.

"You did no such thing," Lilith said sharply, ignoring the sting as she brushed her fingers over Eden's wings. She swallowed hard as their radiance continued to dim, losing their heavenly shine.

"The treaty will hold, though the situation on earth might grow a bit... tense," she said, intentionally understating the situation. There was no precedent set for an Angel murdering one of their own, even in defence.

"I killed her," Eden gasped, her breath coming hard and fast.

"She struck first," Lilith argued, holding the distraught woman closer.

"She just wanted to protect me," Eden said in a wobbly voice, running the scene over and over again in her mind. She could still feel the sudden weight of Gabriel's body as the woman impaled herself on the sword; could still see the shock and hurt in her eyes as Eden chose a demon over one of her own.

"You were never hers to protect, pet," Lilith said firmly.

Truth.

The tears continued to fall, but the demon was devout in her attentions, gently wiping them from Eden's cheeks the second they appeared.

Heaven erupted with fury in the wake of their departure. They called their armies together and rallied their finest warriors to seek retribution for the murder of an Archangel.

But then they realised… they couldn't.

The treaty was intact.

Gabriel didn't fall at the hands of a demon or supernatural entity, not a human or a creature of earth. Her destruction had come from one of their own. There was no precedent to follow; such a thing had never happened before. All they could do was seethe and rage, praying in mass for the fall and damnation of the young Angel who'd betrayed them.

Chapter 14

Eden yawned and pulled the blankets tighter around her body. She reached out, blindly patting the bed in search of Lilith. When she found no trace, she grumbled and reluctantly opened her red-rimmed eyes.

"Is it supposed to be on fire?" She heard, Lilith's voice distinct in its casual flippancy.

Well, that sounded ominous.

"How am I supposed to know?" A slightly higher pitched voice asked in return, signifying Erik's presence.

Eden groaned and pressed her palms to her eyes. For fucks sake. Head pounding, she slowly rose from the bed, still with the blankets wrapped tightly around her body.

She made her way to the kitchen, stopping dead at the sight that greeted her. The hob, for one, was on fire. Of course, it was, why wouldn't it be on fire? How silly of her to assume otherwise, she thought sarcastically.

Several saucepans and frying pans smoked and crackled as the contents smouldered with flame. And before it all, staring down at the carnage in bewilderment, stood Lilith, Erik, and Lucifer.

Just go back to bed, Eden told herself. But then one of the idiots tipped a pan, the oil catching and flame shooting up to the ceiling. The demons just stared at it, completely unbothered by the fire.

Eden bolted forward, turning the knobs and switching off the gas. She backed away from the still flaming pan, massaging the bridge of her nose and internally cursing their very existence.

"Good morning, pet," Lilith said evenly, the sentiment echoed by Erik, who looked far more embarrassed by their predicament.

"I… I can't deal with this right now," Eden said blankly, vaguely gesturing to the fire slowly spreading up the walls.

Lilith tried to speak, only to be halted by a single raised finger. Eden opened the fridge, and once again stopped dead at the sight that greeted her.

No. Absolutely not.

She pulled out a bottle of water, took a long gulp, and swirled it around her mouth.

"In order of *what the actual fuck,*" Eden started, taking in a steadying breath as she pointed at the hob. "Someone put that out. Now!"

When the demons just looked at her dumbly, Eden gestured frantically to the steadily growing fire. Erik clicked his fingers, and it winked out of existence.

"Wonderful. Next up, how fucking dare you show your face here?" She fumed, pointing her finger at the Devil. Eden wondered how much trouble she'd get into for punching Satan in the face. She'd already stabbed an Archangel; it couldn't possibly get any worse.

Lucifer glared back at her belligerently, their ever-shifting face darkening with irritation at the sheer nerve the Angel had to speak to them like that.

Sighing, they looked over to Lilith, who crossed her arms over her chest, staring at them pointedly. "I came to apologise for the very minor role I played in your abduction," they said reluctantly. It was true, but only because of the danger it put Lilith in.

Eden narrowed her eyes.

"And you think that just makes it all magically better? Lilith nearly died because of you. And you call yourself her 'friend," she scoffed, not giving two shits about the steadily sharpening shadows surrounding her.

Her mind was all over the place, muddled and mixed with confusion, anger and fear. Lucifer's tantrums were the last of her worries.

Deciding she had bigger fish to fry, Eden turned her attention to glare at the blonde incubus prodding at the encrusted black remains of a pancake.

"You," she said, pointing at Erik, who blinked at her in confusion, not understanding why he was in trouble.

"The next time someone says, step aside or die. You step aside. Capeesh?" Eden asked sharply, raising her eyebrows expectantly at the man.

Erik nodded his head and winced, half stepping behind Lucifer's ever shifting form as he rubbed his previously broken neck. "You got it, toots," he promised, crossing his fingers behind his back even as he did so.

Eden then turned her eyes to the succubus, who knew exactly what was coming. "And, I can't even believe I have to ask this, but why is there a little ghost girl, in a jar, in the god-damned fridge?" She asked, her voice tired and resigned, unable to believe that this clusterfuck was her life now.

Lilith opened her mouth to respond, only for Eden to wave her hand and cut her off again. "You know what? I'm going back to bed," she said abruptly. "The only person I want to see is Maxx. Bring him back, right now, and clean up this mess."

Eden stalked out of the kitchen, barely stopping to acknowledge the green sludge seeping out of the bottom of the bin. The three demons looked at each other somewhat awkwardly, turning their attention back to their disastrous attempt at breakfast.

"That was a shitty apology," Lilith said, too exhausted to scold them properly.

"She's far more tolerable when angry," Lucy admitted begrudgingly.

"Oh, just get out," she snapped.

Lucifer lingered, hoping to mend the rift they'd created in their longstanding friendship. But Lilith merely glared, lingering fury lighting up her eyes with an iridescent glow. They swallowed hard, sighed, and faded back into the shadows.

"Her wings…" Erik said in a distraught whisper, staring after the Angel. "Has she seen them yet?" He asked, looking up at Lilith with wide eyes.

Lilith swallowed heavily and shook her head. "This is the first time she's gotten out of bed," she admitted, completely lost on how to bring Eden the comfort she so clearly needed.

She pulled a small shard of bone from her pocket and rubbed it slowly. "Who's going to tell her I can't bring back the cat?" She asked, pushing down her own pain at the words.

"Not it," Erik burst out, hastily collecting the burnt pans. He started towards the sink, before realising he hadn't cleaned a single thing in his life, and instead, dumped the whole lot in the bin.

"Fucking coward," Lilith growled, glaring down at the blonde demon.

She made her way back to the bedroom, tentatively poking her head around the door. Eden was once again curled up on the bed, her fading wings stretched out behind her, laying limp over the edge of the frame. Growing bald patches spread over the once radiant appendages, leaving scattered feathers over the bed and floor.

Without speaking, Lilith scooped her into her arms and carried her to the bathroom. She stripped Eden bare, staring helplessly at the woman who was once again lost in a catatonic daze.

The shower sputtered to life, misting over the mirrors and blurring Lilith's reflection as she ran a brush through Eden's hair, endlessly diligent not to snag the numerous matted knots.

She should've done this sooner, she scolded herself.

"My wings," Eden mumbled, her voice blank and a little dazed as she caught sight of them in the misted mirror.

"Have I fallen now?" She asked, looking up for answers.

"No," Lilith said with certainty. "Quite impossibly, you retain your divinity, even now."

"Then why?" Eden probed, pulling the great appendages back into her body with a slight wince.

"Caged birds wilt, pet. And unhappy ones pluck and shed their feathers," Lilith explained, hoping that the analogy would help the Angel understand. Stripping free of her own clothing, Lilith guided Eden into the giant cubical to stand under the gentle spray of the shower, gently running a wet washcloth over her body.

"Where's Maxx?" Eden asked quietly, standing rigid as Lilith cleaned her.

The Demon's hands stilled, her own chest exploding in pain. Not just for Eden, Maxx had been her companion for over sixty years, and his absence felt like a spike to the heart.

"I'm sorry, pet. Animal souls don't follow the same rules as humans or demons. They have to be held here with a vessel; otherwise they just... dissipate into the aether," Lilith choked, wrapping her arms around Eden from behind to rest her hand on the Angel's rounded stomach.

By the time Lilith had made her return to earth, it was far too late to bring the adorable monstrosity back to his undead state.

Eden sniffled and made a pained noise, clinging to the arms holding her steady. "But you can do anything," she snapped, forcibly convincing herself that Lilith just wasn't trying hard enough.

Lilith went quiet.

"I'm sorry, I.." Eden sobbed.

"I know," Lilith murmured, continuing to wash the shaking body under her hands.

"It won't come off," Eden whispered, staring down at her hands as she picked at her nails.

"What won't?" Lilith asked quietly, taking the Angel's hands into her own to inspect them.

"The guilt." Eden shook her head, trying to step out of Lilith's gentle hold as the demon sought to bring her comfort. Lilith held firm, bringing each of Eden's fingers up to her mouth and kissing them.

"Let me take it," she offered, for the hundredth time since their return. There were many creatures with the ability to meddle in the mind, and more than a few owed Lilith their soul, or at the very least, a favour.

Eden shook her head, still feeling cold despite the scolding water running down her back, turning her skin pink and raw.

"How do you do it? You make it look so easy," she whispered hoarsely, slumping down the tiled wall to sit with her knees pressed against her chin.

Lilith sighed and joined her on the floor, lathering shampoo into the Angel's hair. "It is easy. But getting to that point was the hardest thing I've ever done," she confessed, baring a little bit of her own withered soul.

"I don't want to be a monster," Eden shivered, "I don't want to be like you."

Lilith wasn't offended by the insinuation. It was the truth, like it or not. And for the most part, Lilith loved what she was, basked in it even. But Eden wasn't like her; she wouldn't revel in unleashing her darkest, most murderous desires. The Angel was soft, almost unbearably humane, and gentle in a way that was uncommon among supernaturals, light or dark.

"I will always be the monster, so that you don't have to be," she vowed, tipping Eden's head up to seal the promise with a kiss.

While not unbreakable, there was weight in the promise of a demon, a magic that would strain and pull to be fulfilled. After a brief moment of stillness, Eden returned the kiss, pulling Lilith to her and pressing their bodies together.

"Pet, I don't think…" Lilith trailed off, unable to believe that she was refusing sex as Eden's touch grew stronger and more demanding, pleading almost.

"I don't want to think. I don't want to feel. Please I…" Eden stuttered, tears running down her cheeks and mixing with the spray of water. "I want to know only you," she finished, pulling the indecisive succubus closer, clutching and raking her nails down Lilith's pale skin.

As fun as their usual games of cat and mouse were, Lilith was slower this time, more careful as she gaged exactly what Eden needed from her.

"Talk to me," she commanded, standing abruptly and pulling Eden with her, lifting the Angel so that her legs wrapped around her waist as she took them to the bedroom.

Eden was too lost in desperation to speak; she attacked Lilith's neck with her lips and teeth, sinking them into the succubus' skin and leaving deep indented marks.

Lilith growled at the rough motions that were so out of character for Eden, and she harshly threw the Angel onto the bed, pushing her head into the blankets by the nape.

"You *will* talk to me," she hissed, her voice holding more threat than ever before. Not of violence, but rather, it was the threat of withholding her touch, seriously this time, until Eden finally relented and spoke.

She wouldn't risk damaging the girl further.

Lilith pulled Eden's head up, climbing on top of the young woman so that she was straddling her hips.

"Eden," she warned, nipping at the Angel's throat with her fangs but not breaking the skin.

"I want the monster," Eden half sobbed, trying to press her face back into the blankets so that the 'Angel' could disappear, leaving behind the part of her that was only a 'pet.'

Lilith deliberated for a moment, but if this was what Eden needed, then she would give it to her.

"Do you remember your words, pet?" She asked.

Eden nodded, pushing her ass up to rub it against the succubus' pelvis in the hopes that it might sway her desires.

"Say them," Lilith commanded coldly, slamming her flat palm onto Eden's backside. The slap was harsh and sudden, making the Angel jump and cry out at the stinging pain. This was exactly what she needed; Lilith taking away her freedom, her choice, her rights to her own body and pleasure, taking away her guilt and shame.

"G-green, yellow, and red," Eden whispered when she finally found her voice.

"Good girl," Lilith murmured, pressing a kiss to Eden's head, the last gentle touch the Angel would receive until she either passed out or halted their play.

Lilith stood suddenly, backing away from the distraught Angel who reached for her. "Run," she hissed, her glowing blue eyes tracking every slight movement and twitch from the woman before her.

Eden's heart pounded at the predatory command, and she scrambled from the bed to obey. As naked as the day she was born, she ran across the room, and Lilith grinned at the sight of those rounded curves bouncing and jiggling at the hurried movements.

Barely making it to the door, Eden gasped and struggled when Lilith caught her by the hair, using it to drag her back to the bed as she whimpered, and half crawled behind her.

Still fighting the hold, Eden yelled and spat, kicking at Lilith's body as the woman tied her hands and ankles to the bed, the thick leather almost uncomfortably tight as she was forced spread eagle.

Satisfied that the restraints would not break, Lilith stepped back to gaze upon her prey. Tears continuously trickled from Eden's eyes; her chest heaved, pushing her breasts and stomach up and down in time with her frantic breathing.

Lilith drank it all in; the deep dip of Eden's waist, the way her thighs tensed and wobbled, trying to close despite the bindings forcing them to remain spread.

"Colour," she demanded, trailing her black, pointed tail over the arch of Eden's foot, making the Angel squeal and try to jerk away from the tickling touch.

"Green," Eden gasped, quickly responding to her question.

Lilith circled the bed, running her eyes over her pet but not yet touching her. She waited ever so patiently for Eden to break. To beg, to plead, to wish to be destroyed from the inside out.

"Lilly," Eden called to her, the words catching a cry as Lilith whipped her tail over her thighs, leaving long blisteringly red welts across her skin. She'd done it before, but it held a bite this time, a threat of real pain that wouldn't fade with a gentle caress or a kiss.

One of the strikes drew a thin line of blood that welled to the surface, and Lilith bent over Eden's prone form, licking up the tiny amount of blood that began smearing over her skin. She wound her tongue higher to tease, lingering just before the point where Eden's thighs met between her legs.

From one freckle to another, Lilith taunted and denied her with every movement, never straying close enough to bring any real relief.

The Angel tried to buck her hips into the touch; tried to get Lilith where she needed her, only for the Demon to growl and wrap her hand around Eden's throat.

Lilith pressed down, watching closely as Eden's face went red and her mouth gaped, desperately trying to suck in air. She kept it to short bursts, letting the Angel drag in a single gasping breath before applying pressure again.

"Colour?" Lilith checked in, releasing Eden from her grip to reply.

"Green," she wheezed instantly, still coughing and struggling for air even though Lilith was no longer restricting it.

Forgetting herself, Eden pushed on, ignoring Lilith's warning look. "Bite me, please. I want your teeth in my skin," she begged. "I want you to drink my soul dry."

"*My* soul," Lilith corrected. "It belongs to me, remember?" She mocked, poking at the point of her fang with her tongue, drawing a single drop of her own blood.

"Then take it!" Eden demanded, only to release a surprised yelp as Lilith pressed a burning hand to her breast. The fire in her grip was barely hotter than melted candle wax, but the heat engulfing Eden's nipple, swiftly followed by a frosty gust of magic from Lilith's lips, made her quake and convulse, crying out obscenities at the abrupt sensation that bordered on painful.

Lilith pinched at the stiff peaks of Eden's nipples, twisting and tugging on them, grinning wickedly as the woman hissed and tried to wiggle away.

"And do you have any more demands?" She sneered, warming Eden's breast again with a rough squeeze. She bounced the soft globe under her hand, watching it wobble up and down in a way that made the Angel blush and look away as she shook her head.

"Are you going to be a good little fuck toy for me?" Lilith asked darkly, cutting through Eden's restraints with a slash of her claws.

"I thought you wanted a brat?" Eden challenged, intentionally trying to work Lilith into an uncontrolled frenzy to get what she wanted. Complete and total loss of herself to the demon above her.

Lilith smirked.

Sneaky little shit.

Unfortunately for Eden, Lilith had no intention of losing control this time, not when it might come at the risk of seriously hurting her pet.

Anger, magic, and sex, while a sinfully delicious combination, could often walk a fine line between deliriously good, and flat-out dangerous.

"Bratty girls get punished," she laughed coldly, flipping Eden onto her stomach and forcing open her thighs so that she could kneel between them. "But that's what you want, isn't it?" Lilith taunted, pinning Eden's flailing hands above her head with a single hand.

The Angel nodded frantically, more pathetic pleas tumbling from her lips as Lilith rained a series of strikes over her flesh, alternating the location and occasionally rubbing the reddened skin.

Lilith manoeuvred Eden onto her hands and knees, tilting her hips and pressing on her back so that her belly was flush with her upper thighs, displaying her proudly to the succubus.

Using her free hand to spread Eden's cheeks, Lilith moaned as she caught sight of the soaked pink flesh between her legs as well as the darker ring above it. "I hope you remember your colours, pet, because I won't stop for anything else," she said, reminding Eden one more time that she could end their play at any point.

The Angel just whined, trying to push back into the touch that came so teasingly close as endless pleas slipped from her lips.

"So desperately wet for me," Lilith praised, summoning the magical strap and lightly slapping Eden's abused behind as she pushed it inside of her, the Angel's centre greedily swallowing every inch.

Eden moaned, arching her back and pressing her face back into the bed as Lilith gripped her hips, beginning with a series of punishing thrusts that steadily pushed her up the bed.

"You will not come," Lilith ordered, tipping back her head as heat tingled down her spine.

Fuck, she'd missed this. Eden felt divine wrapped around her, clenching the strap, bouncing her hips back to take her deeper.

Eden opened her mouth to argue, only to jolt and widen her eyes as something cold and wet dripped over her exposed forbidden entrance.

"Lilly–" she said uncertainly, trying to wiggle away from the succubus rubbing the lube between her ass cheeks.

"I'm going to fuck both of your holes, pretty girl; turn you into nothing more than a used, broken little thing," Lilith promised, pressing her finger against Eden's asshole and slowly inching her way inside of the virginal cavity, slowing her thrusts to match.

"Wait, wait!" Eden struggled, fresh tears pricking at her eyes at the slightly painful and overwhelming feeling of dual penetration. "Lilly, no!" she cried, and despite Lilith's statement that she wouldn't, she waited for her to become accustomed to the sensation.

"Colour?" She demanded.

Eden gritted her teeth. She wouldn't say it, not for anything. No matter what Lilith did to her, or how much it hurt, she would not cave. "Green," she said shakily.

Lilith paused and frowned, slowly pulling out of Eden completely. She broke their play, only for a minute, to gently kiss the Angel's back. "If you won't say it for *you*, then say it for *me*. Or I stop, right now. I won't risk furthering this if you aren't willing to protect yourself," she said firmly.

Eden's comfort during sex wasn't usually her highest priority, but with the Angel's current state of mind, she wasn't leaving anything to chance. No matter how much her darker impulses pressed for her to make good on her promise to take Eden until she was broken and bloody.

After a long moment of silence, the Angel finally spoke. "Yellow," she admitted through a sobbing hiccup. "But please don't stop; I want it," she whispered, turning her head to look up at her with pleading eyes.

"If you lie to me again…" Lilith trailed off, narrowing her eyes on the Angel below her.

"I won't, I promise," Eden vowed, frantically nodding her head and trying to push herself back onto the strap prodding at her thigh.

Their play resumed, and Eden sucked in a sharp breath as Lilith's finger slowly pressed into her alongside the magical phallus.

After several minutes of tense gasps and startled sounds of pain, Eden slowly began to relax into the double penetration, pushing back into the thrusts with a guttural moan.

"That's it, pet. Can you feel what your pretty little pussy does to me?" Lilith taunted, her own voice brimming with ecstasy as her pleasure built. "Whose ass is this, Angel?" she demanded, striking her with her free hand.

"Fuck, yours!"

Harder. Faster. The punishing sound of skin against skin echoed through the apartment, with every piercing thrust followed by a sharp cry from the Angel baring all to the succubus behind her.

"Please can I cum?" Eden pleaded, "please, please." Her impending orgasm threatened to shatter what remaining restraint and dignity she had left. "I can't hold it."

"You will," Lilith said heatedly, twisting the finger in Eden's behind, withdrawing completely before plunging in with a second. A shattered scream met her actions, and Lilith laughed as she jogged her hips against the Angel's backside in time with her fingers.

Lilith praised her over and over, completely contrasting every abuse she inflicted as she whipped her tail over the girl's back, eliciting more tortured cries that flicked between overwhelming pleasure and pain.

Lilith talked her through every second, and although her words were sweet, the succubus somehow managed to make them sound like the most degrading things in the world.

A wave of something heady and dizzying swept over Eden. She felt light, floaty even, as her abused body turned to mush under Lilith's hands. The pain lessened to barely anything, leaving only pleasure and a desperate need to please and obey. Like an out of body experience, Eden felt like she was watching her domination through the eyes of someone else as she disappeared completely inside of herself, leaving only a thrall who existed to serve.

"Mistress," she moaned in a breathy whine, her shaking body slumping further into the bed.

Lilith held her in place, momentarily stunned by the title that evoked a fresh, feverish rise of desire in her core. Half of the demons in existence referred to her as such, but from Eden's sweetly pink lips, it was different.

More intimate and trusting.

Lilith promised herself that she would be worthy of the title. "Oh, my treasure," she whispered in astonished realisation. She made sure to keep the same pace; the same frequency of strikes along Eden's skin, not increasing the force of her thrusts as the Angel slipped into sub space. There was no greater gift that Eden could've given her. No wonder that could've compared to the complete trust and control that she'd just handed over.

"You are perfection, made only for me."

Truth

Eden was too lost in pleasure to register Lilith's words, as well as the response they pulled from her powers. Especially when Lilith's tail halted its strikes to gently flick against her clit.

"Cum for me, pretty girl."

The release that was previously denied floated up and down Eden's body. Time stood still, centring on the relentless throbbing between her legs that pulsated and spread to engulf her entire form.

There were no Angels or Demons, no Heaven or Hell. There was only Lilith. Eyes rolling back into her head, Eden convulsed, collapsing back onto the bed as she went completely limp.

Lilith gave a short, disbelieving laugh, transitioning her thrusts into a steady grind as she lingered on the cusp of her own orgasm. With a deep groan, she tensed and released, coming undone inside of Eden's fluttering walls. Resting her weight on the Angel's back, she took a moment to catch her breath before beginning to pull the magical strap out.

"Stay," Eden slurred, without the strength to so much as lift her head.

Lilith hesitated before smiling, carefully turning them so that she was positioned behind Eden with their bodies still connected in the most intimate of ways.

"Lilly," Eden whispered beseechingly, her body trembling as she began to crash and fall from her high. Tears gathered on her lashes and her hands fisted in the quilt below, bunching it between her fingers.

"Hush, I've got you, pet. You did such a good job," Lilith said softly, running her hands over every available inch of Eden's skin as a comforting purr vibrated in her chest.

They lay there for hours, and even when Eden slipped into sleep, Lilith continued stroking her body, kissing and whispering into her hair with words of dark devotion slipping from her lips.

Chapter 15

Eden smiled and pressed a kiss to Lilith's neck from her place on the woman's lap. They were holding 'court' in the newly built Devil's Dealings. Though it was called 'Eden's Paradise' now, something that made her blush every time she heard it, as 'paradise' was what Lilith often moaned as she sunk into her.

Eden didn't dare ask what happened to the old club, nor did she ask why the new one remained so empty for the first few months after opening. But whatever had happened, the supernatural world seemed to have a short memory, because it was soon teaming with all sorts of degenerates looking for cheap, trashy entertainment.

With the ever-present threat of Heaven's retribution, progress for Eden was slow. But surely enough, she was slowly regaining her spark. Something that made all those around her breathe a heavy sigh of relief.

When Lilith was the cheeriest person in the room, it was incredibly disconcerting. Especially for Erik, who had been forcibly moved into the veritable skyscraper by his sire and reluctant maker. Apparently getting murdered had gained him one too many brownie points, because the bloody woman wouldn't leave him the fuck alone. And while Erik had longed for nothing more than her attention his entire life, the dour overprotectiveness was getting pretty annoying.

"You know, we can all smell you," he leaned in to whisper.

Eden blushed and peeked out of Lilith's hair to glare at the impish man. "One more word, and I'll tell the new waiter he's your screensaver," she threatened, pointing a pink tipped finger at the incubus.

"I'm surrounded by children," Lilith sighed irritably, even as her eyes flickered with amusement. She squeezed Eden's waist, softening the statement further.

Eden hummed and pulled back. "Speaking of children, you have got to find some way to stop Lizzie from poking her freaky little ghost head through the bedroom door," she said lightly, a bemused laugh falling from her mouth even as a faint grimace twisted on her lips. "Oh, and Erik wants a new car."

"Erik has a car," Lilith said dryly, intentionally ignoring the rest of Eden's demands. Souls were incredibly empathetic things, and until Lilith found a way to give Lizzie a new body, the ghost constantly trailed behind Eden like a little lost puppy.

Apparently, keeping her in a jar was 'child abuse,' despite the fact she was already dead. Eden also wouldn't allow her to stuff the girl into a doll or some other inanimate object as she had originally planned. Lilith wisely kept from revealing that her own car's *ever so shining personality* came from the soul it housed.

"A better car," Erik chimed in, not so cowed with his angelic protector around. Financially speaking, getting his neck snapped for the woman was probably the best thing he'd ever done.

"A better car," Eden reiterated, unable to fight the slight tugging on her lips that threatened to stretch into a full-blown grin.

"Cars don't come cheap," Lilith said slyly, opening the situation up to a little extortion.

Eden nearly broke into giggles.

"Please, you have absolutely no idea how much they cost. You were surprised that milk no longer cost a half penny when I dragged you shopping," she accused.

"At least she didn't try paying with gold bars or a bucket of salt," Erik snarked, winking at Eden as they tag-teamed the succubus.

Lilith exhaled deeply through her nose, narrowing her eyes on the mischievous duo. "*You* will find yourself vacationing in Hell for an interminable amount of time if you don't go and find someone else's tail to tug. I summoned your soul here; I can banish it back just like *that*," she griped, snapping her fingers for emphasis as she glared down at the incubus.

Erik laughed a little nervously and retreated to the bar with a sarcastic bow to his mistress.

"I regret bringing that little rat back every second," Lilith muttered.

Lie.

Eden resisted the urge to counter Lilith's words. They'd made an agreement that she wouldn't use her powers against the demon, even in play. If Lilith wanted to delude herself a little, then Eden would merely roll her eyes and let it pass.

She would always know the truth anyway.

"And you…" Lilith trailed off, eyeing the doe eyed Angel who was biting her lip to keep from smiling.

Eden cocked her head and looked up to her innocently. "Yes?" She asked sweetly.

Lilith huffed out a laugh and curled a finger through Eden's hair, tugging on it just enough to sting. "You are perfect," she conceded with a small smile.

Eden preened and straightened up under the assessment, only for her smile to drop at Lilith's next words.

"Very well, Erik may have his car. On the condition that you get one too," the succubus bargained.

Eden crossed her arms over her chest and frowned, tapping Lilith's chin to draw the woman's attention away from her breasts.

"A second-hand car," she countered.

Lilith made a sound of amusement and wound her tail between Eden's legs, lifting the dress to stroke along her thighs. "Top of the line, newest model, reclining seats, and tinted windows so I can fuck you if we get stuck in traffic," she said firmly, unwilling to budge on the matter. Never mind the fact that tinted windows were illegal in the UK. Money bought a lot of things, the mortal police turning a blind eye being one of them.

Eden bit her lip to keep from moaning as Lilith's tail ventured higher. She clamped her legs closed, trapping the appendage between her thighs.

"I don't even know how to drive," she protested breathlessly, blushing fiercely and squirming as the eyes of dozens of demons swivelled to look at them.

Lilith grinned deviously, her blood-red lips mere millimetres from Eden's ear.

"Don't you worry, pet, I'll teach you. I'm sure you'll be an expert at riding stick in no time," she teased.

Eden rolled her eyes and laughed. "That was awful, even for you."

Lilith shrugged, tucking the girl back into her neck and returning her eyes to the demons below. A noiseless snarl split her lips as she warned them to avert their eyes from her most prized possession. They did so, quickly fleeing from her gaze as they sought out entertainment that would not result in their heads being removed from their person.

Erik shortly returned with a tray full of drinks, a scrap of paper with a phone number on it stuffed between his pretty lips. Eden teased him mercilessly, poking and prodding at his sides, pulling on his tail just as she did when she made fun of the demon beneath her.

Lilith stayed quiet, content to watch as the pair bickered and played, constantly fighting for the upper hand. Snippets of her fractured friendship with Lucy came to mind, and Lilith stifled her grief at the breaking of the timeless pact.

They had repeatedly tried to apologise, to regain her favour and trust, but passed the single apology she'd forced them to give to Eden, she'd rebuked all efforts they'd made to rekindle their bond. Going so far as to toss their coin back into Hell and seal the portal behind it.

Raising a hand, Lilith brushed her fingers over the small shard of bone on the end of her necklace. Maxx's absence sat heavy and alarmingly present at all times, but Lilith did her best to focus on the family growing before her eyes.

"I love you," she whispered out of the blue, her iridescent eyes glowing with the weight of the thousands of souls who echoed her statement.

Eden paused mid-sentence to look up at her. "I love you too," she said, her face a perfect mirror of Lilith's adoration as she gazed at the monster who'd claimed her.

Epilogue

The creator looked upon the world, seeing the good, the bad, the pure, and the wicked. All of which were symbolised in the union between an Angel and a Demon.

Plans were unfolding, a little haphazardly in places, but unfolding, nonetheless.

Author's note

Thank you so much, and I hope you all enjoyed reading this as much as I enjoyed writing it. If you are interested in reading more of Eden and Lilith's story, then please follow along for more. I would be eternally grateful if you could leave a review or comment to let me know what you think. The first few lit a happy fire in my soul, and the wife likes to laugh at my silly dance moves as I celebrate.

About the Author

Mia M.R is a budding Author who loves to read and write lesbian romance stories. Anything with Dragons, Witches, or Mermaids is right up her alley. Bonus points if it has a little extra steam. ;-)

Mia married her wife in 2022, and they are currently the crazy cat ladies on the street. You can follow her through Amazon, Goodreads, TikTok, and Facebook under Mia M.R - Author.

(You should definitely check out my TikTok account. I post some really cringey shit.)

Also by Mia M.R

The Fall of Angels: Dark Sapphic Romance (The Heart of a Demon Book 3)

A woman's fear isn't weakness, it's kindling. Fuel for the fires of rage that will never stop burning.

Retribution isn't always swift. But Lilith knows all too well the horrors that those who claim to be 'good' and 'pure' can inflict.

When the forces of Heaven fall to seek revenge for the murder of the Archangel Gabriel, Lilith's restraint over her monstrous instincts is put to the test.

Will Eden seek to escape Lilith's grasp to preserve her own life, or will she allow herself to be consumed, falling prey to the very creature she swore her soul to?

Printed in Great Britain
by Amazon